BRUTAL VENGEANCE

Center Point
Large Print

Also by J. A. Johnstone and available from
Center Point Large Print:

The Big Gundown
Seven Days to Die
Rattlesnake Valley
The Bounty Killers
Trail of Blood
Killer Poker
The Blood of Renegades
Crossfire
Inferno

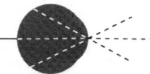

**This Large Print Book carries the
Seal of Approval of N.A.V.H.**

The Loner:
BRUTAL
VENGEANCE

J. A.
Johnstone

CENTER POINT LARGE PRINT
THORNDIKE, MAINE

This Center Point Large Print edition is published
in the year 2015 by arrangement with
Kensington Publishing Corp.

Copyright © 2012 by J. A. Johnstone.

The text of this Large Print edition is unabridged.
In other aspects, this book may vary
from the original edition.
Printed in the United States of America
on permanent paper.
Set in 16-point Times New Roman type.

ISBN: 978-1-62899-525-1

Library of Congress Cataloging-in-Publication Data

Johnstone, J. A.
  Brutal vengeance : the loner / J. A. Johnstone. —
    Center Point Large Print edition.
    pages cm
  Summary: "When he is rescued from a bloody West Texas gun battle
by a beautiful bounty hunter, the Loner, a quiet kid with a lightning fast
gun, is led into another fight for survival that could be his last"—
Provided by publisher.
  ISBN 978-1-62899-525-1 (library binding : alk. paper)
  1. Women bounty hunters—Fiction. 2. Large type books. I. Title.
  PS3610.O43B78 2015
  813'.6—dc23
                                                        2014049685

BRUTAL
VENGEANCE

CHAPTER 1

Dusk was settling down over the West Texas town of Fire Hill as Vint Reilly walked home from the stage station.

The day had been blistering hot, as usual, but now that the sun was down the dry air was beginning to cool. The faint breeze felt good on his face as he glanced toward the knob west of town.

The founder of Fire Hill, old Marcus Burton, had come to these parts forty years earlier, not long before the Civil War, to start a ranch. He'd figured he wanted a town as well, to supply the needs of that ranch. The spot on the stream that came to be known as Burton Creek had been a good choice for the settlement.

According to legend, Marcus Burton had stood at that spot and looked toward the knob just as the sun was setting behind it. The red glare made it look like a giant fire was burning on top of the hill. It had impressed Burton a lot, so he'd dubbed the new town Fire Hill, Texas.

The citizens still knew it by that name.

Old Marcus was still around. His M-B Connected ranch was the largest in that part of the state.

Reilly had a lot on his mind because of Marcus

Burton. The old man had had a sizable amount of cash shipped in. Since the closest railroad station was sixty-five miles south of Fire Hill, the money had arrived on the three-times-weekly stage.

Reilly had been running the stage station for five years. The satchel full of bound bundles of greenbacks was now locked in the safe in his office. It was the most money he'd ever had in that old safe.

It made him nervous. He didn't know why in blazes Burton couldn't have had somebody meet the stage and take the cash back out to the ranch.

Reilly had asked Burton that question when he came into town to arrange the shipment.

"I do things in my own time," the crotchety old cattleman had insisted. "My men are busy, can't just take off to run around willy-nilly. I'll have somebody here to pick it up in three or four days."

In the meantime Reilly was stuck with the responsibility of making sure the money stayed safe. Burton didn't seem to understand that . . . or more likely, just didn't care.

Reilly had hired Tom Rodman and Peter Donahue to stand guard over the money at night. Donahue was young but pretty tough, a part-time deputy for town marshal Alonzo Hyde. Rodman was getting up in years, but had worked for the stage line as a shotgun guard for a long time before the bouncing of those Concord coaches had gotten to be too much for his aching bones. Reilly had confidence in both men.

But he still wished that money was somewhere else besides his safe.

He would walk back down to the office after supper and check on the guards, he decided. His wife Delores was fixing pot roast—one of his favorites—and he wasn't going to miss out on it because of some stubborn old man.

Turning in at the gate in the fence around his front yard, he could already smell the delicious aroma of the meat drifting from his house. A smile tugged at his mouth.

He glanced again at the hill that had given the settlement its name. For some reason he couldn't fathom, his smile disappeared and a worried frown creased his forehead.

Damn Marcus Burton anyway, Vint Reilly thought.

On top of the hill overlooking the town sat forty men on horseback. Their leader, Warren Latch, was at the edge of the slope, slightly in front of the other men.

He was hatless, and the wind stirred his long brown hair. The jutting beard he wore was the same shade. A Mexican serape rested on his shoulders and draped down over his chest and back. Under it were crossed bandoliers of 7.63mm ammunition for the matched pair of Mauser C96 semi-automatic pistols he wore in flap holsters at his waist.

He had ordered the pistols 'specially from Germany. Being able to kill swiftly and efficiently was very important to Warren Latch, and the Mausers gave him a deadly edge that not many men possessed.

One of the other men edged his horse up alongside Latch's mount. "It's getting to be along toward time, Warren."

"Not yet," Latch said. "I want it to be good and dark before we go down there. In the time those pathetic fools have left, I want them to shiver in fear of the horrors that descend on man out of the endless night. I want to be their worst nightmare, Duval, the kind that sends them screaming out of sleep . . . and out of this life!"

Slim Duval shrugged. He didn't care about any of that. He only cared about the big pile of Marcus Burton's money sitting in that stage station's cracker-box safe.

Fortunately, Latch cared about that, too, no matter how much he liked to rant about other things. In the end, he would see to it they got the money and everything else they could loot from the town of Fire Hill. That was all that mattered.

As his name implied, Slim Duval was a slender man. He was something of a dandy as well, always dapperly dressed in a black suit and Stetson, with a diamond stickpin holding down his silk cravat. He was a Cajun, though he'd long since lost the accent.

He'd been a gambler in New Orleans and on the Mississippi riverboats before those halcyon days had drawn to a close. When they did, he had drifted west and fallen in with Warren Latch, discovering he was as equally talented as a desperado as he was with a deck of cards.

Duval had been Latch's second-in-command for a while, the only member of the gang who was close to the long-haired boss outlaw. "You sure the money's there?"

Latch jerked his head sharply toward his lieutenant. "If it's not, Jed Miller will die slowly and very painfully for lying to me."

Miller was the clerk who worked in the railroad shipping office and fed information to Latch about the best targets for the gang's robberies.

"Miller might not have lied," Duval pointed out. "But he could have made a mistake."

"Then he'll die for making a mistake," Latch snapped. "But whether the money's there or not, by morning the town will be nothing more than smoldering heaps of rubble."

"Fine," Duval said under his breath. He knew good and well that Latch was loco. The man lived for death and destruction.

But riding with him sure paid well.

As the last of the light from the sunset faded out of the sky, Latch peered down hungrily at the settlement. To himself as much to anyone else, he said, "Soon. Very soon."

Vint Reilly stood up and went around the table to rest his hands on the shoulders of his pretty, olive-skinned wife. Delores turned her head to smile up at him. "Good?"

"*Muy bueno*," he told her in the language of her people.

She laughed. "You don't have to speak Spanish to me. You know that, Vint."

"I like to. The words are beautiful. You're beautiful. And it's a beautiful evening."

"Which you're going to spoil by going back down to the station to sit *there* with Tom and Peter when you could be spending time *here* with your loving wife."

Reilly groaned. "You're tormenting me, woman. It's not like I'd rather be there. I'm just worried about that money."

"Why should you be?" Delores asked. "Obviously, Marcus Burton isn't, or he would have had some of his men in town to pick it up when the stage came in."

"I told him the same thing," Reilly said, "but you know how he is."

Delores sniffed. "Stubborn as an old mule?"

"That's about the size of it." Reilly smiled. He leaned over farther, rubbed his cheek against his wife's velvety cheek, and kissed the glossy black curls on her head. "I won't be gone long. Once I've seen for myself that Tom and Pete have everything under control, I'm sure my nerves will settle down, and then I'll come on home."

"Those nerves of yours had better not take too long." Passionate lights twinkled in Delores's dark eyes. "If they do, I'm liable to be asleep when you get back."

"Wouldn't want that." Reilly chuckled as he straightened.

He went to the front door as Delores got up and started clearing the table. Reilly took down the Winchester hanging on the wall and snagged his flat-crowned hat from its hook. He settled it on his tightly curled brown hair and smiled at his wife. "See you later."

"Don't be long," she warned again as she carried empty plates into the kitchen.

Reilly sighed as he left the house. He had taken reasonable precautions to protect Marcus Burton's money. Most men would have said the hell with it. If anything happened, it would be Burton's fault, not his.

The rancher wouldn't see it that way, though, and likely Reilly's employers at the stage line wouldn't, either. He tucked the Winchester under his arm, opened the gate, and headed for the station.

It was too dark now to see the hill west of town.

CHAPTER 2

Kid Morgan reined his buckskin to a halt, and the pack horse he was leading stopped, too. He had ridden longer than he'd intended to, until after dark. He'd had some trouble finding a spot to camp that suited him.

The gravelly shelf alongside a narrow stream would have to do. A little bluff backed up to it, but the terrain on the other side of the creek leveled off into a flat stretching for miles. The Kid wouldn't have to worry about flash floods, although such occurrences were rare in West Texas.

He swung down from his saddle and picketed both animals so they could reach the water, then took the saddle off the buckskin and untied the packs from the other horse. The moon wasn't up yet, but the millions of stars overhead provided enough light for him to see what he was doing.

There was plenty of dry brush around to provide fuel for a small fire, but maybe it would be a better idea to make a cold camp, The Kid thought. Lighting any sort of fire in the vast plains would announce his presence, and he wasn't sure he wanted to do that.

It hadn't been very long since he'd clashed with some renegade Apaches who had come up over the border from Mexico to raid. One dustup like that was enough.

The Kid spread his bedroll and positioned his saddle to serve as a pillow. Taking a coiled hair rope from his gear, he laid it out in a circle around the place he would sleep. That would keep any curious rattlesnakes from trying to crawl into his blankets with him. His father had taught him that trick.

Frank Morgan, the notorious gunfighter known as The Drifter, had taught The Kid a lot of things, but not how to use the Colt that rode holstered on his hip. That skill had come to him naturally. Likely he had possessed it all along, although he might not have ever discovered it if his wife had not been murdered and if he hadn't set out on the vengeance trail.

Those days were long gone now. Tragedy had dogged The Kid's steps again and again, until finally, he had put everything from his previous existence behind him. From here on out, he rode alone.

That was the plan, anyway.

Fate always seemed to have other ideas.

He dug some jerky out of his packs, along with a couple biscuits left over from his breakfast that morning. It was a pretty sparse supper, and a far cry from the gourmet fare he had once enjoyed as a rich, spoiled young man.

But it would fill his belly, at least partially, and

that was all The Kid cared about right then. He sat down cross-legged on his bedroll, set his hat beside his saddle, and pulled off his boots. Then he ate his meager meal as he listened to the tiny noises of small animals moving around in the brush. The night was so quiet he was able to hear the swish of wings as an owl swooped down, then the squeal of fear and pain as the predator plucked up a desert mouse for its supper.

Always death, The Kid thought as he slowly chewed a piece of jerky. Even in the middle of all this peace and quiet, always death.

Peter Donahue was tall and gawky, with a shock of blond hair and buck teeth. His nose had been broken somewhere along the way and had healed crookedly. He was a part-time deputy with a quick, charming smile. When a fight broke out in the Swingin' Door Saloon, he could usually calm down the troublemakers just by talking to them.

But when he had to, he could wallop somebody with his big, knobby fists, and he was a fair hand with a gun, too.

Tom Rodman was a head shorter than his fellow guard and seemingly an ax handle wider, although that was just an illusion because Rodman was so stockily built. His hair was almost completely gray and his jowls had started to sag a little, giving him the appearance of a bulldog.

However, no bulldog had ever been able to

handle a double-barreled Greener like Rodman. During his years as a stagecoach guard, he had blasted half a dozen road agents out of their saddles.

Through one of the station's front windows, Vint Reilly saw the two men sitting at a table, playing dominos. He rapped on the glass to get their attention so they wouldn't be spooked when he unlocked the door and went in. Rodman looked up, saw him, and nodded a greeting. Donahue grinned.

"Everything quiet?" Reilly asked as he stepped into the station.

"As a church mouse," Donahue replied with his customary grin.

"Didn't expect to see you back tonight, Vint," Rodman drawled as he shuffled the dominos. "That's why you hired Pete and me to look after the place."

"Yeah, if I had me a pretty little wife like Vint does, I'd be home sparkin' her right now," Donahue added.

"If you think I'd rather be here with you two pelicans than home with Delores, you're loco. I just got to worrying and thought I'd see how you were doing. I won't stay long."

"No need for you to stay at all." Rodman pushed the dominos toward Donahue, his movements curt and impatient. He seemed to think that Reilly was questioning his and

Donahue's ability to guard Marcus Burton's money. "Half the town's asleep already, and except for a few folks down at the Swingin' Door, the other half soon will be."

"I'm not worried about the people here in Fire Hill," Reilly said.

"You shouldn't be worried at all," Donahue said. "Nobody knows about the money, do they?"

"Nobody's supposed to know about the money. That's not quite the same thing."

Reilly was right about that. The officials at the railroad and the stage line had tried to keep the details of the shipment quiet, he knew, but when large amounts of money were involved, news had a way of leaking out.

"You gonna get your dominos or not?" Rodman asked Donahue.

"I'm gettin' 'em, I'm gettin' 'em," the younger man said as he drew nine of the rectangular pieces toward him. "Hold your horses, Gran'pa."

Rodman snorted.

Donahue grinned. "You reckon I'll get any count this time? You been givin' me bad dominos all night."

"Bad dominos, my hind foot! You've had double-five every time. It's your turn to down."

Donahue set his dominos up so he could see them. He paused, picked one up, and placed it faceup in the center of the table. "Wouldn't want to break tradition," he said as he moved the peg in his little scorekeeping board.

Rodman grunted and shook his head. He said something about dumb luck under his breath, but that just made Donahue's grin grow wider.

They weren't worried, Reilly told himself. There was no reason he should be. Donahue was right. He should be home with Delores. "Looks like you boys have got everything squared away here."

"Darn right we do." Rodman placed a domino on the table. "Let's see you make something out of that."

"It just so happens I can make fifteen." Donahue gleefully swooped a hand in to place a domino of his own. "You shouldn't have forgot that double-five's the spinner, Tom."

Rodman groaned.

Chuckling, Reilly let himself out of the office. He paused on the boardwalk to listen to the night instead of turning back immediately to lock the door behind him.

At first the only sound he heard was the faint tinkle of player piano music coming from the saloon at the other end of the street.

Then something else intruded on the peacefulness. A low rumble, like thunder over the mountains or the sound of distant drums.

Reilly stepped to the edge of the porch and looked up at the sky, thinking a storm might be brewing. The region was mostly arid, but sometimes a summer thunderstorm could blow up seemingly out of nowhere.

Not tonight, Reilly decided. From horizon to horizon, the sky was clear. Everywhere he looked, more stars than he could hope to count in a lifetime sparkled against the sable backdrop of the heavens.

There were no Indians in these parts—the cavalry had pushed the few remaining Apaches far down into the Big Bend to the southwest—so the sound couldn't be drums, either. Apaches didn't really use drums in their preparations for war, anyway.

With those two explanations ruled out and the sound growing louder, Reilly had to ask himself what he was hearing.

There was only one answer, he realized as he stiffened with alarm.

He wheeled around and plunged back into the office, startling Donahue and Rodman.

"Horses coming fast!" Reilly said. "A lot of them!"

Duval urged his horse forward, trying to keep up with Latch as the outlaw leader galloped toward Fire Hill. It was difficult to match his pace whenever he charged into battle.

More than once, Duval had thought Latch had been born out of his time. He should have been around during the War of Northern Aggression, a conflict Duval had studied quite a bit. Latch would have made a perfect cavalry commander for the Confederacy: dashing, brave, more than a little mad. Duval could imagine him at the head of a whole regiment of southern boys, attacking the Yankees in the face of overwhelming odds, never giving up, fighting to the end.

But Latch had missed his chance for glory. Instead he was an outlaw and a cold-blooded killer. His mania had been redirected to other ends.

Might as well make a profit off it, was the way Duval looked at the situation.

The scattered lights ahead of them showed that only about half the town was still up. A lot of Fire Hill's citizens were already asleep in their beds.

Soon their peaceful slumber would be rudely disturbed. They would be jolted out of sleep by screams and gunshots and would run out to see what was going on, only to meet their own death. It was inevitable.

Eagerly leaning forward over his horse's neck, Warren Latch turned his head to howl an order at his men. "Kill everything that moves! Kill them all!"

CHAPTER 3

Tom Rodman and Pete Donahue stood up quickly from the table where they had been playing dominos. Donahue's rifle was lying on the desk, and Rodman's shotgun hung on the wall. Both men grabbed their weapons.

"Just because riders are comin', it doesn't have to mean anything, Vint," Rodman said.

"The hell it doesn't!" Reilly hurried to the desk and blew out the lamp. "You know better, Tom."

"Maybe old man Burton decided to send some of his cowboys to pick up the money after all," Donahue suggested as darkness enveloped the office. "That might be all it is."

"From the sound of those hoofbeats, he would have had to send his entire crew, and I don't think he'd do that." Reilly's voice was grim as he went on, "No, boys, that's trouble coming. I'm sure of it."

"If it is, we'll give trouble a warm welcome," Rodman vowed. "Pete, take the window on the left. Vint, you take the right. I'll plant myself right in front of the safe."

Reilly didn't argue. Tom Rodman had fought a lot more outlaws than he ever had. Reilly had fired a gun in anger only twice in his life, both times at Comanches who had raided his father's ranch up in central Texas when Reilly was a teenager. The Comanches had come to steal horses, but both times Reilly and his pa and his brothers had driven them away.

Reilly didn't know if his shots had hit anybody during those fights. It was certainly possible. And he had no doubts about being able to shoot at any varmints who tried to steal the money from the safe. He didn't want to kill anybody, but he would if he had to in order to do his job.

"Steady, boys," Rodman said into the darkness. He sounded calm, a lot calmer than Reilly, whose heart was pounding so hard he thought it would burst out of his chest. "Once some slugs start buzzing around their heads, those owlhoots will probably turn tail and run."

Reilly hoped the older man was right.

He'd raised the window to the right of the door. Donahue had done the same on the left. Both men knelt with their Winchesters thrust out through the openings. Reilly could still hear the thundering hoofbeats, although the roaring of blood inside his head threatened to drown them out.

The riders were coming from the wrong direction to be the M-B Connected crew, he realized. Burton's ranch was north of the settlement. These men were riding in from the west, from the direction of the hill.

Had they been up there earlier when he was looking at it? Reilly couldn't help wondering.

Had danger been lurking up there even then?

No matter. It was here now.

The riders swept into town at the western end of Main Street. Gunshots slammed out immediately as the men opened fire. Reilly leaned forward to peer out the window as muzzle flashes lit up the night in a weird shadow show. He saw a man who'd been walking along the boardwalk on the opposite side of the street suddenly crumple, riddled by bullets.

The bastards were shooting at anything that moved, Reilly realized wildly. They hadn't come just to steal the money at the stage station. They were there to loot the whole town.

"Get 'em, Pete!" he cried as he pointed his rifle at the onrushing horde and pulled the trigger.

Donahue's Winchester cracked a split second after Reilly's did. Reilly worked his rifle's lever and fired again. A storm of lead smashed into the stage station in response. The outlaws saw the muzzle flashes from Reilly's and Donahue's Winchesters and concentrated their fire on the station.

The windowpanes above Reilly shattered into a million pieces as several bullets struck them at once. Razor-sharp shards of glass sprayed across the office and down over him. He ducked his head so his hat protected his face to a certain extent, but he still felt the sting on his hands and the back of his neck.

Behind him, Tom Rodman yelled furiously, "Those sons of bitches!"

"Get down!" Reilly shouted as slugs began to punch through the plank walls. "Get down on the floor!"

He flattened out and hoped Rodman and Donahue did the same. The walls stopped some of the bullets, but not enough of them. Deadly chunks of lead zipped through the air in the room. Their high-pitched whine was an ugly sound.

Donahue grunted. "Damn."

"Pete! Are you hit?"

"Yeah. Not too bad, though. Bullet went through my left forearm. I can still hold my rifle."

"Tom, how about you?" Reilly raised his voice to be heard over the gun thunder from outside.

"I'm all right so far," Rodman said. "What in blazes are they doin'?"

The racket slacked off slightly. Reilly raised his head and risked a quick look out the window. "They've gone past us. They're down at the other end of town now, shooting it up."

"What're they gonna do?" Donahue asked. "Ride back and forth shooting like crazy men until they've shot up every building in town?"

Reilly suddenly realized there was a very good chance the men would do just that. "This isn't just a robbery. It's a raid, like an attack on a town during a war. They'll kill as many people as they can."

"We gotta stop 'em!" Donahue began struggling to his feet.

"Three of us against more than a dozen of them?" Reilly hadn't been able to tell exactly how many outlaws there were as they charged past the stage station, but he knew he and his companions were badly outnumbered.

"We can whittle down the odds the next time they charge us," Rodman said, "and I know just how to do it."

Before Reilly could ask the old shotgun guard what he meant, Donahue cried out, "You're gonna get your chance, Tom! Here they come again!"

Rodman lurched up from the floor. He started toward the door as Reilly said, "Tom, what are you—"

"Outlaws are cowards!" Rodman said as he jerked the door open. "Give some of 'em a faceful of buckshot, and the rest will run!"

He stepped out onto the porch before Reilly could stop him.

"Eat lead, you buzzards!" Rodman bellowed as he brought up the Greener.

His finger hadn't tightened on the triggers when at least half a dozen slugs thudded into his body, driving him back toward the door. The impact made the shotgun's barrels rise higher as he finally jerked the triggers and sent both barrels harmlessly into the wooden awning over the boardwalk.

Rodman crashed down on his back, his upper body inside the office and his legs still on the porch. "Jesus, Mary, and Jo—"

That was all he got out before a strangled gasp choked him, and Reilly knew his friend was dead. Rodman's foolish attack hadn't accomplished anything except to get him killed.

The shooting continued outside. Reilly and Donahue managed to get off a few rounds in return, but the fierce barrage from the gang's guns forced them to the floor again. Bullets whined around them.

"Oh, hell!" Donahue said. "I'm hit again."

Some providence had protected Reilly so far, although he didn't see how. He crawled toward Donahue, wincing as some of the glass slivers covering the floor poked through his clothes and sliced into his flesh. "I'm coming, Pete. I'm coming to get you."

"Hell, no!" Donahue gasped. "Get out of here, Vint! You can't stop 'em. Let 'em have the damn money. Go out the back and save yourself!"

"I won't leave you here—" Reilly's words stopped short as the shooting outside slacked off again. He heard something else, a terrible crackling and roaring, and as he glanced through the open door where Tom Rodman's body lay, he saw the reflection of a flickering, orange-tinted glare.

The smell of smoke drifted to his nose a second

later. It was different from the acrid tang of the gunsmoke filling the night.

That was wood burning, Reilly thought. A building going up in flames, from the look of the light outside.

The bastards were putting the town to the torch!

"Go," Pete Donahue said again, his voice weak. "You gotta get to . . . Delores . . ."

Fear stabbed deep into Reilly's guts. His wife was at home alone, and even if the outlaws hadn't gotten around to his house yet, sooner or later they would. He had to reach Delores, get her out of there. They could flee on foot into the darkness. It was a cowardly thing to do, but it might save her life.

That was more important to Reilly than anything else.

"Pete, I'm sorry—"

"Don't be . . . Just stop flappin' . . . your gums and . . . rattle your hocks . . . outta here." Donahue got a hand under him and pushed himself into a sitting position. His rifle lay across his lap. "I'll keep 'em . . . busy."

Grunting with the effort, Donahue lifted the Winchester and started firing through the open door at the shapes on horseback darting back and forth in the street.

The nightmarish glare outside had grown brighter. More buildings were ablaze.

The station didn't have a back door, but there

was a window at the end of the hall past the storeroom where Reilly could get out. He started in that direction, but as he reached the hall he paused for a final look back at Donahue.

It wasn't his wounded friend who caught his attention, though. It was one of the riders in the street. The man wore a long duster but no hat. Long hair hung loose around his shoulders, and a beard jutted from his jaw. The glare from the conflagration washed over him as he hauled back on his reins and forced his horse to rear.

The look on the man's face as he turned his head toward the stage station was like nothing Vint Reilly had ever seen before. It was pure madness, pure evil, like looking into the face of Satan himself.

Reilly knew he would never forget that face as long as he lived.

Pete Donahue triggered a shot at the man, but his strength had all but deserted him, and the Winchester's barrel sagged, sending the slug into the boardwalk outside the door.

The outlaw brought his mount down and raised his hand. In it was some sort of funny-looking pistol with an odd grip and a big magazine where a revolver's cylinder would normally be.

Fire licked from the weapon's muzzle as bullets poured out of it, as fast as the killer could squeeze the trigger. The slugs stitched into Donahue's body, making him jerk and twitch.

It was the last thing Reilly saw inside the station. He turned and plunged through the darkened hallway. Lowering his head and holding his Winchester in front of him, he crashed through the window at the far end. He was already cut up. A few more gashes wouldn't mean anything.

In a shower of broken glass and splintered window frame, he burst out of the station and fell to the ground behind the building. The hard landing knocked the breath out of him. Gasping for air, he forced himself to his feet.

He had to get home before it was too late. He started along the alley behind the buildings in a stumbling run as screams, gunshots, and the crackling roar of Fire Hill's destruction filled the night.

CHAPTER 4

Kid Morgan turned over in his bedroll. His eyes opened, and instantly every sense was alert.

He had the ability only a few men possessed, that of emerging from a sound sleep fully awake and ready for trouble. Without thinking about reaching for a gun, his hand was already wrapped around the walnut grips of his Colt.

He lay motionless, listening intently and letting his gaze roam around the campsite to see as much as he could from where he was.

He sniffed the air, searching for the smell of unwashed human flesh or the lingering odor of tobacco smoke.

Nothing.

He risked turning his head enough to look at the buckskin and the pack horse. Both animals were dozing. The Kid didn't expect any sort of vigilance from the stolid pack horse, but the buckskin would have been spooked if anybody or anything was nearby that shouldn't be.

He sat up slowly. The night around him was as peaceful and quiet as it could be.

Maybe he'd only had a dream, he told himself. Perhaps a nightmare he couldn't remember had jolted him out of sleep.

That was unlikely, though. If it wasn't, he might be going loco. Lord knew, with everything that had happened in the past two years, he had reason enough to lose his mind.

The Kid stood up and stretched, turning toward the north. His movements stopped suddenly.

The terrain was mostly flat in that direction, and far, far away, he saw a tiny glow, low on the horizon.

Something was burning over yonder, he thought, bringing back memories of a wagon train he had encountered recently, over in New Mexico Territory. He had seen the light from the wagons burning in the night, too. He had gone to investigate and found death, tragedy, and trouble that had drawn him in and nearly ended his own life.

Whatever was burning, it was none of his business. He could tell it was a good-sized fire, but it was long miles away. Even if he saddled up and headed in that direction as fast as the buckskin could carry him, he would be too late. He couldn't get there until long after whatever was happening was over.

He wondered if that was what had roused him. Had some instinct told him there was trouble going on somewhere else, and that he needed to be there?

That was a crazy idea, he told himself. He wanted to avoid trouble, not find it. He didn't even want to be around people any more than he had to.

For a while, anyway. Maybe that would change someday, but for now he wanted to ride lonesome.

He bent and slid the Colt back into its holster. The buckskin raised its head and nickered sleepily.

"It's nothing," The Kid told the horse. "Go back to sleep."

He hoped he could take his own advice.

The outlaws had started burning the town at its eastern end, probably because they didn't want the stage station going up in flames before they had a chance to get in there and steal Marcus Burton's money. The safe would probably protect the cash, even if the building burned down around it, but the gang wouldn't want to risk losing the money.

Those were the thoughts going through Reilly's head as he hurried frantically toward his house. The stage station was located toward the western end of Main Street, and his home was farther west.

The house he shared with Delores was one of the first the raiders had charged past as they entered Fire Hill. He wondered if she had heard the hoofbeats and if the sound had frightened her.

No doubt she had heard all the shooting, and was probably terrified, more for him than for herself, though. She was smart enough to know Burton's money was most likely the reason those evil men had come to Fire Hill. She would be scared something had happened to her husband.

Well, it had come close, mighty close, Reilly thought. It was sheer luck he hadn't died in that stage station, too.

Or maybe his life had been spared for a reason. Maybe he had lived so he could save Delores. That thought made him feel a little better about taking her and running for their lives.

Horses pounded past on Main Street, heading west again. Men whooped.

Not men, Reilly amended.

Monsters.

That's what they were, monsters in human form, and that long-haired bastard in the duster was the worst of the lot, Reilly told himself. He didn't know how he knew that, but the conclusion was clear in his mind.

He shoved that thought away. Another minute and he'd be home.

Suddenly, he saw flames shooting into the air. "Noooo!"

The outlaws had set fire to the buildings on the western end of town. The flames would burn toward each other and wipe out the entire settlement.

Reilly ran faster. His only hope was to get to his house before the fires spread that far.

That hope was dashed cruelly as he came in sight of his house. Livid red and orange flames were already shooting from the roof and out the windows. He threw aside his Winchester, not wanting anything to weigh him down as he sprinted frantically toward his home.

Men rode past and shot at him, but he only vaguely heard the bullets whistling past his head. His only thoughts were for Delores. He might still have time to reach her . . .

The fire was burning most fiercely on the front side of the house, where the raiders had thrown their torches to set the place ablaze. Reilly headed for the back door, slowing just long enough to lift his right foot and send it crashing against the door just above the knob. The door burst open.

Terrible heat slammed against his face like a

physical blow. Smoke swirled around him, choking and blinding him. He stumbled forward as he was seized by a fit of coughing.

"Delores!" he managed to shout, hoping she had gotten out before the outlaws set fire to the house. "Delores, where are you?"

It was only a few steps to the desert. Reilly really wanted to believe she could have fled into the night, but he didn't think it was what she would have done. She would have stayed, thinking he would come for her.

Well, he had. Now he just had to find her.

Moving through the house was like being trapped in a nightmare where he had gone to hell. Smoke and flames were everywhere. The trappings of his life were being destroyed all around him, but he didn't care about any of that.

All he cared about was Delores. He called her name again and again, his voice becoming more hoarse and pain-wracked with every shout. Catching sight of a human form lying slumped on the living room floor, he threw himself toward it, screaming, "Delores!"

He fell to his knees beside her, reaching out to grab her shoulders and roll her over to pull her into his arms and carry her out of the inferno.

Her head lolled loosely on her neck as he turned her. Reilly sobbed, a deep, gut-wrenching sound, as he saw her face in the hellish glare of the fire. A black hole marred her smooth forehead, and below it her wide eyes stared sightlessly.

One of the wild bullets fired by the outlaws had come through a window or maybe even through the wall and struck Delores, killing her instantly.

Reilly pulled her limp form against him as violent shudders shook him. He couldn't believe it, couldn't bear to let her go.

He pressed his face into the thick waves of her hair, trying to inhale as much of its scent as he could. But the smoke that seared his nostrils was the only thing he could smell.

A crash close by startled him out of his grief-stricken stupor. The roof was starting to come down.

He didn't care anymore whether he lived or died, but he couldn't leave Delores there to burn. Gathering her against him, he struggled to his feet and turned toward the kitchen, intending to make it out the back of the house with her.

"Vint! Vint! Are you in there?"

The shouts barely penetrated his consciousness. He looked toward the back door and saw someone standing there. Smoke wreathed around the man, who coughed and pressed a bandanna over his face in a feeble attempt to block out some of it. When the man moved the bandanna, Reilly recognized the craggy features of Marshal Alonzo Hyde.

"Come on, Vint!" Hyde cried when he spotted the stage station manager emerging from the smoke. "You can make it!"

But Reilly couldn't. More of the roof fell, coming down like a sheet of flame between him and Hyde.

As he recoiled from it, a great weight struck him in the back and knocked him off his feet. He cradled Delores against him as he fell, even though she was past feeling any pain, ever again.

Sheer, stubborn determination made Reilly struggle to get up. Suddenly all the strength flowed out of him like water from an overturned bucket. He couldn't move anymore.

He lay there, coughing as the smoke filled his lungs and the flames began to eat at his flesh. He couldn't even scream at the searing agony.

Red hell surrounded him, then faded to black.

CHAPTER 5

Several days after waking up in the middle of the night and seeing the distant glow of the large fire, Kid Morgan was easing his buckskin down a long, rugged slope separating the plains behind him from the plains in front of him. The drop was a couple of hundred feet.

This escarpment was bound to have a name of some sort, The Kid thought. Not being that familiar with the geography of the Lone Star State, he had no idea what it was.

He had been taking it easy, not getting in any

hurry as he traveled across West Texas. The long, leisurely days tended to blend together. He didn't give much thought to how much time had passed since the night something had disturbed his sleep. It hadn't happened again, and he had pretty much put the disquieting incident out of his mind.

The buckskin was sure-footed, so The Kid let the horse pick its own path down the slope. Time and the elements had seamed and scored the ground until it resembled the face of an old man. Boulders littered the escarpment, and it was dotted with clumps of hardy brush.

Snakes could be hiding in that brush, seeking its shade to escape the heat of the day. The Kid knew how common rattlers were in this godforsaken part of the country. South and west of there was a place called Rattlesnake Valley where he had run into a considerable amount of trouble a year or so earlier.

Nothing spooked a horse faster or more completely than the fierce buzzing of a diamondback's rattles. If the buckskin or the pack horse started jumping around on the slope, it could lead to a disastrous tumble.

So The Kid was ready for trouble . . . just not for somebody shooting at him.

The flat crack of a rifle shot came from somewhere to his left, followed by a high-pitched whine as the bullet ricocheted off a nearby rock. The Kid yanked the buckskin to a halt and jerked around in the saddle to look toward the source of the shot.

He saw several men riding along the edge of the escarpment a couple hundred yards in that direction. A cloud of dust trailed behind them.

More shots rang out as powdersmoke spurted from their rifle barrels. The men turned their horses down the slope and started angling along the escarpment's face toward him.

The Kid looked around quickly. No big rocks were close enough to provide cover, but down at the base of the slope, where the ground leveled out again into seemingly endless plains, several giant slabs of stone had come to rest after breaking off and sliding down the escarpment in ages past.

"Let's go!" The Kid kicked the buckskin into a bounding run.

The caution he had been using was forgotten. It was obvious those men wanted his hide, preferably with several bullet holes in it. He'd have to figure out why they wanted to kill him once he reached the rocks.

The buckskin leaped from rock to rock. The pack horse wasn't nearly as nimble, and The Kid knew the animal couldn't hope to keep up. He let go of the reins. Under the circumstances, he would rather lose the pack horse and the supplies it carried than have it slow him down.

Supplies wouldn't do him any good if he was dead.

Bullets continued to ricochet off the rocks around him, but he wasn't far from the bottom of the slope. Frustrated shouts came from the men pursuing him, afraid he was going to reach those stone slabs and fort up. Then they would have trouble getting to him.

That was exactly what The Kid planned to do. He could have pulled his Winchester from the saddle boot and returned their fire as soon as they started shooting at him, but he knew he had a better chance of survival if he got off the rugged escarpment.

The buckskin's hooves slid on some loose gravel. For a second The Kid's heart pounded harder in his chest as he thought the horse was going down.

An excited yell erupted from one of the pursuers as he saw the horse struggling, but the buckskin regained its footing and continued the headlong charge down the slope, reaching the rocks without falling and breaking its neck. Neither The Kid nor his mount had been hit by any of the bullets whipping around them.

Pulling his rifle from its scabbard, The Kid kicked his feet free of the stirrups, and left the saddle in a leap. He landed running, almost lost his balance, then regained it and dashed behind one of the giant stone slabs.

The buckskin kept going. That was fine with The Kid. The horse was a good one, and he wanted it out of the line of fire.

Taking a deep breath, he pressed his back against the rock for a moment as he waited for his racing pulse to slow. When it had, he stepped to the corner of the slab, brought the Winchester swiftly to his shoulder, and cranked off three rounds as fast as he could work the repeater's lever.

He aimed high, over the heads of the men who were chasing him, deciding not to blow the varmints out of their saddles . . . for now.

He didn't like killing anybody without knowing the reason why.

Of course, the fact that they had tried to kill him first was reason enough to respond with deadly force, he supposed, but he was curious. He didn't know anybody in this part of Texas who would want him dead. He didn't know anybody in this part of Texas, period.

Somebody had made a mistake, and it sure wasn't him.

The bullets cutting through the air a few feet above their heads were enough to make the men think twice about continuing to charge The Kid's position. They hauled back on their reins and whirled their horses around.

The turn was too sharp for one man's mount. The horse lost its footing and went over with a shrill, terrified whinny. The man on its back screamed, too, as he was thrown from the saddle.

From where he was, The Kid couldn't tell if the

horse had rolled over on the man, crushing him. He didn't particularly care. He might not be willing to shoot them just yet, but if one came to a bad end because of his own ineptitude, it served him right.

He had not had time to count the pursuers. Now that he had reached cover, The Kid saw there were four. Three of the men were still on their horses. Two were fleeing, but the other one hesitated.

"Clyde!" The Kid heard him shout. "Hang on! I'll get you, Clyde!"

That had to be the name of the man who had fallen from his horse. The Kid saw him scramble to his feet as the other man reined his horse in that direction. He was going to pick up Clyde and let him ride double.

The Kid lined his sights and fired. The slug whistled between the two men, coming close enough that Clyde yelped and instinctively leaped backward. He tripped and landed on his butt.

The Kid fired again, chipping rock from the ground near the hooves of the mounted man's horse.

The man hauled hard on the reins and whirled his horse, turning away from his fallen comrade.

"Damn it, Hogan!" Clyde yelled as he leaped to his feet. "Don't leave me here!"

Hogan didn't pay any attention to him. He was out to save his own skin.

The Kid worked the Winchester's lever and sent

another round over Clyde's head, close enough to make the man throw himself facedown on the slope. There was no cover around him. Even his horse was gone, having run off after its fall, seemingly unhurt.

Clyde was an easy target. All he could do was lie there, cover his head with his arms, and wait for the smashing impact of the bullet that would end his life.

The Kid held his fire.

Two men had already vanished over the top of the escarpment. Hogan followed them, his horse lunging over the rim and carrying him out of sight. That left The Kid and Clyde alone with the hot Texas sun beating down around them.

Several minutes of near-silence passed. The only things The Kid could hear were the faint sighing of the hot wind and the terrified whimpers coming from Clyde.

Finally, the man lifted his head slightly and called, "P-please don't kill me, mister! I can't do nothin' to hurt you now! Please don't kill me!"

The Kid leaned a shoulder against the rock and didn't say anything. He waited.

Another minute passed. Clyde raised his head a little higher, enough to look around. He was starting to think The Kid was gone. Putting his hands under him, he pushed himself up.

The Kid sent a bullet slamming into the ground five feet in front of him.

Clyde screamed and bellied down again.

He wouldn't be trying to move again any time soon, The Kid guessed. He knew he was being a little cruel, but he was mad. He'd been riding along, not bothering anybody, not looking for trouble, and suddenly those men were shooting at him. He didn't like it, and Clyde was paying for the anger he felt.

"Hey, mister!"

The shout floated down from the top of the escarpment. The Kid was expecting it. More than likely the others had crept back up to the rim and peered carefully over it. They could see that Clyde was still alive and that The Kid had him pinned down.

With the giant slab of rock in the way, they couldn't get a good shot at The Kid. Now would come the talking.

"Hey, mister, can you hear me?"

"I hear you!" The Kid called back. "What do you want?"

"You let our man go, so he can walk back up here to us!"

"So you can all start trying to kill me again?" The Kid laughed, even though the sound probably didn't carry all the way to the top of the escarpment. "I don't think so!"

"Look, those boys went off half-cocked when they spotted you!" the man shouted. "I'm sorry about that! They thought you were one of the

44

buzzards we've been chasin' the past few days!"

Well, that made things a little more interesting, assuming the man was telling the truth, The Kid thought. From the sound of it, the man doing the talking wasn't one of the four who had tried to kill him. Maybe now he could find out what was going on here.

"Who are you?"

"Texas Ranger!" the unseen man replied. "Name of Asa Culhane!"

A Ranger, The Kid thought. That made sense, he supposed. A Ranger leading a posse of some sort, and they had split up to scout for whoever they were after. Clyde and his friends had spotted The Kid and jumped the gun . . .

Yeah, it could have happened that way, but The Kid wanted to be sure. A man who took another man's word too easily, sight unseen, often wound up dead.

"Clyde!" he called to the man lying on the ground. "I know you can hear me, Clyde!"

The hapless Clyde had his arms crossed protectively over his head again and his face pressed to the ground. He lifted it slightly and said, "Y-yeah?"

"Is that fella at the top of the slope telling the truth, Clyde? Is he really a Texas Ranger?" The Kid paused. "If I think you're lying to me, I'll kill you, you know that."

"It's true!" Clyde practically screamed. "He's a

45

Ranger! His name's Culhane, just like he said!"

The Kid smiled thinly. "All right, Clyde, I believe you. But you just stay right where you are for now, anyway."

"How about it, mister?" the voice called from the top of the escarpment.

The Kid made up his mind. "Come on down, Culhane!" he shouted. "But just you! We'll talk."

CHAPTER 6

After a moment, a man on horseback appeared at the top of the slope. He started down toward The Kid, in no rush. He let his horse pick its way carefully, the same way The Kid had been descending from the escarpment before all the shooting started.

The Kid was careful to stay back where the rock gave him cover, just in case the other members of the posse were spreading out up there and trying to find an angle where they could get a good shot at him.

As the rider came closer, The Kid saw that he was a big, barrel-chested man in his forties. Clean-shaven, with the sort of tanned, weathered face that said he had spent most of his life outdoors. He wore a black Stetson tilted back a little on his head, and a black vest over a gray shirt.

Pinned to that shirt was a silver star set in a silver circle. The Kid knew that was the badge of the Texas Rangers.

But anybody could wear a badge, so The Kid didn't trust the man fully just yet. When the rider was about twenty feet away, The Kid said, "That's close enough."

The man reined in, keeping both hands in plain sight. "Take it easy, mister. If you ain't part of Latch's gang, then we don't want any trouble with you."

"Shooting at a man is a funny way of showing that. And I never heard of anybody called Latch."

"You're lucky, then, and even luckier if you never crossed his path. Warren Latch is just about as close to the Devil in human form as you're ever gonna find. I said I was sorry about the shootin'. If you ever rode with a posse before, you know how things can get outta hand plumb easy."

The Kid didn't respond to that. "You said your name is Culhane?"

"That's right. Asa Culhane. Originally from Jacksboro, Texas. You know any of the Jacksboro Culhanes?"

"Not that I recall," The Kid said dryly. "You have any identification besides that badge, Culhane?"

"If you'll let me reach in my pocket without shootin' me, I'll be glad to show you my bona fides."

"Go ahead." The Kid peered at Culhane over the barrel of his Winchester. "Just do it slow and easy."

Culhane followed that order, reaching carefully under his vest into a shirt pocket. He pulled out a thin leather folder and tossed it toward the rock. It fell almost at The Kid's feet.

A thin smile tugged at The Kid's mouth. "Now I bend over to pick that up and you go for your gun, is that how this is supposed to work?"

"I'm just tryin' to give you what you asked for, mister," Culhane said.

"Get your hands high. I'm not going to make it easy for you."

Culhane shrugged and lifted his hands as high above his head as his arms could reach. Without taking his eyes off the Ranger, The Kid bent at the knees and held the Winchester with one hand as he reached down with the other for the leather folder.

When he had it, he straightened again. He flipped the folder open and glanced at the card and the folded papers inside. They identified the bearer as Asa Culhane, a Texas Ranger attached to Company C in San Antonio.

"All right, put your hands down." The Kid didn't see any point in being needlessly stubborn. He closed the folder and tossed it back to Culhane, who caught it easily. "Let's say I believe you're really a Ranger."

"Good . . . because that's what I am." Culhane's eyes narrowed as he tucked away the folder in his pocket. "You mind lowerin' that repeater, son? Havin' it pointin' at me like that makes me a mite nervous."

The Kid aimed the Winchester at the ground between them. He could lift it again in a hurry if he needed to.

"Come on around behind this rock with me, Culhane," he said. "That way we can talk without me worrying about some of your men trying to pick me off from up there."

"They're not gonna take any more potshots at you. I gave 'em strict orders not to open fire unless I told 'em to."

"Yeah, well, you probably told them not to go around trying to murder anybody they happened to come across, too, and look how well they followed those orders."

Culhane laughed. "I reckon you got a point there, son." He turned his head toward the man on the ground. "Clyde! Get back up there and tell the rest of the boys I said no more shootin' unless they're shot at first. If anybody gets trigger-happy again, I'll kick his ass from here to Texarkana, personal-like!"

Clyde hesitated. He called to The Kid, "Is . . . is it all right if I get up, mister?"

"Go on," The Kid said. "Deliver Ranger Culhane's message for him."

That put an end to Clyde's hesitation. He scrambled to his feet and ran up the slope, slipping and staggering from rock to rock in his haste. The Kid could hear him panting from the exertion.

"All right, Culhane," The Kid went on. "Get down from that horse and come around here."

"That bit about not gettin' trigger-happy goes for you, too, you know." Culhane swung down from the saddle and let the reins dangle so the horse, if it was well-trained, would stay where it was. Keeping his empty hands in plain sight, Culhane walked around the massive stone slab.

The Kid backed away, watching intently for any telltale signs that Culhane was about to make a grab for the holstered revolver with staghorn grips he wore on his hip. The Ranger kept his hands half raised.

"Reckon the first thing we better clear up is who you are, amigo," Culhane said when he was behind the rock.

"No, the first thing we need to get clear is that if any of your men try to sneak up and pull something funny, you'll die. I'll see to that."

"I believe you." Culhane nodded. "But believe me, those boys ain't gonna try nothin'. You got 'em plenty spooked. Reckon you could've killed Clyde and those other three without much trouble, and they know it."

The Kid sensed that Culhane was telling the

truth. He didn't really want to be on the bad side of the Texas Rangers. They were a legendary organization, probably the West's most famous outlaw hunters, and once a man's name was written down in their book, they never stopped pursuing him.

"That's right, I could have killed them, but I didn't, because I'm not one of the men you're looking for. My name's Morgan. I'm just passing through these parts."

"Morgan, Morgan . . ." Culhane mused. "Don't recall seein' that name on any reward dodgers lately."

"That's because I'm not wanted," The Kid said.

That hadn't always been the case. For a while there had been a bounty on his head in New Mexico Territory, but that was a mistake and had been all cleared up.

"You got nothin' to worry about from us, then. We're after a gang of desperados led by a man named Warren Latch."

"I told you, I never heard of him. What did they do?"

Culhane's rugged face took on a bleak cast. "A few nights ago they raided a town northwest of here called Fire Hill. Name's fittin', because they burned the place to the ground and killed a bunch of folks in the process. They were after a shipment of cash that was bein' held in the safe at the stage station."

"There are still stagecoach lines around here?"

"The railroad don't go everywhere just yet."

In his previous life as wealthy businessman Conrad Browning, The Kid had built numerous spur lines, but he knew Culhane was right. Some settlements were too small to make running the steel rails to them profitable.

"Latch is the sort of outlaw who's kill-crazy," the Ranger went on. "He wasn't just tryin' to steal that money. He wanted to loot as much else as he could from the town and then destroy it and the folks who lived there. Came pretty close to doin' it, too. Only one or two buildin's were still standin' when I got there. The rest were just ashes."

That was the fire he had seen several nights earlier, The Kid thought. It had to be. The glow was large enough to have been an entire settlement going up in flames.

"Only about a hundred people lived there," Culhane continued, "and more'n half of 'em were killed in the raid, either by bullets or by the fires Latch's men started."

"How do you know it was Latch's gang that was responsible?" The Kid asked. The grim story had caught his interest, despite his continuing resolve not to get mixed up in any trouble.

"Some of the survivors got a good look at him," Culhane explained. "This ain't the first job Latch's bunch has pulled. They've held up trains and robbed banks all over West Texas, and we've got a good description of him. The senseless killin' matches what he's done in the past, too, although I got to say he outdid himself this time. He never tried to wipe out a whole town before."

"If this only happened a few nights ago, they got the Rangers on the job pretty fast," The Kid commented.

"That's because I happened to be in Fort Stockton on some other law business when a rider come gallopin' in the next mornin' with the news of what had happened. I wired my cap'n in San Antonio and told him about it, and he said for me to rattle my hocks over there as fast as I could and try to pick up Latch's trail. Some of the men from town who could ride wanted to come with me, and as it turns out, the cattleman whose money got stole from the stage station was puttin' together a posse, too. So I sort of combined everything and took command."

"How many men do you have?"

"Twenty-four, countin' me." Culhane smiled, but there was no humor in the expression. "And before you ask, Latch's bunch is forty or fifty strong, so I'm mighty glad you didn't ventilate any of my boys. We're already outnumbered. The odds don't need to be any worse than they already are."

Culhane was more than outnumbered, The Kid thought. Considering what Latch's men had done to the town of Fire Hill, they had to be hardened killers. A bunch of store clerks and cowboys wouldn't be any match for them.

Culhane might have been thinking the same thing. He regarded The Kid with a shrewd, intent expression. "You got the look of a fightin' man about you, Morgan. I'm sure sorry for the little misunderstandin' we had, and I'd be mighty happy if you was to throw in with us—"

"Forget it." Hearing about what Latch's gang had done at Fire Hill outraged The Kid's sense of justice . . . but that sense had taken a beating over the past couple years. Along with a helping hand from Fate, he had brought justice to the people responsible for his wife's murder . . . but Rebel was still dead, wasn't she? Going after Warren Latch wouldn't bring the people he had killed in Fire Hill back to life, either.

"I could sure use the help," Culhane tried again.

The Kid was about to shake his head and tell the Ranger to go back to the posse, while he rounded up the buckskin and pack horse and rode in the opposite direction as fast as he could. He would have stuck to that decision, too . . .

If gunfire hadn't suddenly erupted at the top of the escarpment.

CHAPTER 7

Culhane jerked his head in that direction as he reached for the gun on his hip. "Son of a—"

"Hold it!" The Kid snapped as he leveled the Winchester at the Texas Ranger. "If this is some kind of trick—"

"No trick," Culhane said. "I swear to you, none of those posse men would try anything. It sounds to me like somebody else jumped 'em!"

Culhane had a point. The shooting continued, fast and furious. The Kid had been in enough gun battles to know the real thing when he heard it.

"Damn it, Morgan, I need to get back up there!"

The Kid nodded. "Go ahead. I'll come with you." He didn't know where the offer came from. Volunteering to help the posse had been the furthest thing from his mind only moments earlier.

But something about the sound of gunshots drew him. He had a difficult time turning away while bullets were flying.

Culhane ran around the rock, grabbed his horse, and mounted in a hurry. The Kid's buckskin and pack horse had drifted onto the flats to graze on the sparse grass. He didn't take the time to go after them. He followed Culhane on foot, leaping agilely from rock to rock, carrying his rifle.

Since the slope was so rugged, The Kid climbed

it almost as fast as Culhane did on horseback. Looking up, he saw men scrambling over the rim and dropping below it for cover. They turned and fired back toward the west.

Culhane noticed that, too. He reined in before he reached the top and dropped out of the saddle, dragging his rifle from its sheath. He went to his knees at the rim and peered over.

A second later, his black hat leaped from his head and went flying into the air.

"Great jumpin' Jehosophat!" Culhane yelled. Reaching up, he felt his head as if he couldn't believe his hat was gone.

The Kid knelt beside him. "Are you hit?"

"No, but one of the blasted varmints sure as blazes ventilated my hat!"

Even under the circumstances, The Kid had to chuckle at Culhane's indignation. The Ranger had come within bare inches of having his brains splattered all over the landscape, and he was worried about his hat.

Or maybe that was just his way of not thinking about how close he had come to death.

Angrily, Culhane thrust the barrel of his Winchester over the rim and triggered a couple swift shots before ducking back down again.

"Marchman!" he yelled at one of the posse members ranged along the ragged brink of the escarpment. "Any of our men been killed yet?"

The man shook his head and called back,

56

"We've got a couple wounded, but nobody's dead!"

"Let's try to keep it that way!" Culhane urged.

The Kid spotted Clyde not far off. The man kept shooting nervous glances toward him. To Culhane The Kid said, "You'd better make sure those fellas know that I'm on your side now."

"Are you, Morgan?" Culhane asked. "On our side, I mean?"

"For now," The Kid said with a nod.

To prove it, he slid his rifle over the rim and sighted on the dozen or so horsebackers who were throwing lead at the posse. They were riding back and forth about a hundred yards away, apparently untouched. The men from Fire Hill couldn't draw a bead on moving targets.

That wasn't the case with Kid Morgan. He settled his cheek against the smooth wood of the Winchester's stock and squeezed the trigger. The rifle cracked, and one of the bushwhackers jerked in the saddle and started to slide off his horse. The man managed to grab his saddle horn and stay mounted, but he slumped far over in obvious pain as he turned his horse and galloped farther away.

Several of the posse men let out exultant whoops.

"We got one of the buzzards!" a man shouted.

Culhane looked knowingly at The Kid. The Ranger was well aware who had winged that outlaw. "Hold your fire and listen to me!" he shouted. When he had the men's attention, he went on, "This fella with me is Morgan! He's not one of Latch's men after all. He's throwin' in with us!"

The members of the posse didn't celebrate that news, but some of them nodded in acknowledgment of it. The Kid felt more confident that at least they wouldn't turn on him at the first opportunity.

"Now pepper those damned bushwhackers, and pepper 'em good!" Culhane ordered.

The shooting resumed. The Kid squeezed off another shot and saw a man's arm jerk. A round from Culhane's rifle made another man's hat fly from his head.

"Turnabout's fair play!" the Ranger said with satisfaction.

He and The Kid seemed to be the only ones scoring any hits, but after a few minutes that was enough. The riders stopped shooting, turned their horses, and spurred away, putting ground between themselves and the posse as fast as they could.

Seeing that, some of the posse members started to stand up, no doubt figuring they were safe.

"Blast it, stay down!" Culhane bellowed at them. "There may be some sharpshooter out there with a long-range rifle just waitin' for you woolly sheep to stand up and take a bullet through the head!"

The men dropped back into cover along the ragged edge of the escarpment as The Kid's estimation of Culhane's abilities grew. Obviously, this wasn't the Ranger's first dance.

"That was some good shootin' you done," Culhane said to him. "You can handle a Winchester. How are you with that short gun on your hip?"

"I get the job done," The Kid said.

In truth, he was one of the fastest and deadliest pistoleers left on the frontier, his skill with a Colt probably exceeded only by his father, Frank Morgan.

"I'll just bet you do," Culhane said with a nod. "And I'm glad you're with us now, instead of against us, Morgan."

The men crouched and knelt there, sweating in the heat, for a good ten minutes longer before Culhane said, "All right, I reckon it's safe to move around again. Some of you hombres start roundin' up those horses."

The Kid saw a number of saddle horses scattered across the plains along the edge of the escarpment. It was easy enough to figure out what had happened.

The posse had been dismounted, watching the confrontation at the bottom of the slope instead of paying attention to what was behind them. The outlaws jumped them, stampeding the horses and forcing the men to scramble for cover.

Culhane waved one of the men over to him. "Marchman, what in blazes happened up here?" he demanded.

"It's not our fault, Ranger," the man replied in a surly voice. "They hit us from behind, when we weren't looking."

"Of course they did! They figured a bunch of greenhorns like you wouldn't have enough sense to keep an eye on your back trail . . . and they were right!"

Marchman glared. He was a short, thick-bodied man in town clothes. He wore a narrow-brimmed hat that he took off in order to wipe sweat from his flushed face and mostly bald head with a bandanna. "This isn't a troop of Rangers you're talking to, Culhane."

"Don't forget that we're volunteers."

Culhane grunted disgustedly. "I ain't likely to forget you fellas ain't Rangers. Rangers wouldn't have got took by surprise and bushwhacked that way."

Marchman's broad face flushed with anger. "I'm gonna go see to the wounded."

"You do that," Culhane told him. "Make yourself useful."

Marchman strode off.

When the man was gone, The Kid commented, "Rode him a little hard, didn't you?"

"Yeah, and I reckon I know better." Culhane sighed. "I just get mighty frustrated with the

60

whole bunch. It ain't easy trackin' down a gang like Latch's with a bunch of storekeepers and forty-a-month punchers."

The comment unwittingly echoed what The Kid had thought earlier. He let his gaze roam over the members of the posse, and didn't like what he saw.

About half of them were townsmen from Fire Hill. Business owners, clerks, bartenders, and the like, he assumed.

The rest were cowboys, some of them so young they might not be out of their teens. A few of those ranch hands might be fairly tough and competent, but not enough to match up with a gang of ruthless outlaws.

Clyde and Hogan were townies. They hovered close to Marchman as the burly man used strips of cloth torn from a shirt to bind up a man's wounded arm.

Culhane saw where The Kid was looking. "Ed Marchman owned the general store in Fire Hill. Clyde Fenner clerked for him, and Jack Hogan drove the wagon that brought in the merchandise Marchman sold. I reckon they're all three out of a job now, since the store's gone. The fella who got shot through the arm is Woody Anderson, Fire Hill's blacksmith. Same goes for him."

Culhane pointed out several of the other men and told The Kid their names. The Kid knew he wouldn't remember most of them, but nodded anyway.

One of the young punchers came up to them. "Ranger Culhane, I can't find my horse."

"Well, keep lookin', boy," Culhane said. "Maybe one of your grandpa's hands will find it if you can't."

"All right." The youngster nodded. He was undersized, with a freckled face and a shock of red hair.

As the young cowboy moved off, Culhane said quietly, "That's Nick Burton, old Marcus Burton's grandson."

Culhane said the name like he expected The Kid to know who Marcus Burton was, but The Kid didn't have any idea and said as much.

"Burton's the owner of the M-B Connected, the biggest spread in these parts," Culhane explained. "It was his money Latch was after. Burton sent some of his men after the outlaws, and the kid came along with 'em."

"Was that his idea, or his grandfather's?"

Culhane snorted. "It was the old man's idea. Claimed he wanted to have a member of the family represented on the posse, so he saddled me with the boy. Nick can at least ride, and he claims he can shoot, but I got a hunch he's gonna be more hindrance than help in the long run. I needed those M-B Connected hands to come along, so I agreed to it."

Before Culhane could say anything else about the members of his posse, a man came up behind them and rasped, "We're wasting time, Culhane. We need to get after them."

The Kid looked over his shoulder at the new-comer . . .

And saw something out of a nightmare.

CHAPTER 8

The man had been horribly burned, that much was obvious at first glance. The skin visible on his face was red and raw. Strips of cloth, criss-crossed here and there, were wrapped around his head as bandages, covering the worst of the burns. Ugly yellow stains marked where pus from leaking sores had soaked through.

The Kid could tell from the way the bandages lay flat against the right side of the man's head that his ear was completely gone. Part of his nose looked like a lumpy, roasted potato that had been left in the fire too long.

He wore a hat, but it sat awkwardly on the bandages covering the top of his head. His hands were thinly wrapped, so he could still carry the rifle he had with him. The Kid saw more bandages peeking out through gaps between the man's shirt buttons and speculated that most of his body was swathed in cloth.

A man this badly injured belonged in a hospital, not out riding with a posse through the wilds of West Texas.

"Well, how about it?" he said in a tortured croak. "Are we going after them or not?"

"We're goin', Mr. Reilly, but we can't leave until everybody's rounded up their horses," Culhane said.

"I've got my horse," Reilly said. "If I can catch him, you'd think these others could round up their mounts."

"You're sure right about that. I reckon it won't be much longer now."

Reilly shook his head balefully and turned away. The Kid noticed the other men moved back to give him room as he walked through the posse toward the horses that had been gathered so far.

"Ain't that the most pitiful thing you ever saw in all your born days?" Culhane asked.

"You weren't as sharp with him as you were with the others," The Kid pointed out.

"Well, how in Sam Hill could I be? You saw the way the fella looks, and you don't even know the whole story!"

"What is it?"

Looking at the burned man, Culhane said, "His name's Vint Reilly. He ran the stage station in Fire Hill."

"So it was his safe Burton's money was in."

The Ranger nodded. "That's right. I reckon he feels some responsible for what happened, although when you come right down to it, there's not a blessed thing he could've done to stop it.

He and a couple guards were at the station when Latch's gang hit town. The other two hombres were killed almost right away. Reilly got out and headed for his house."

"He abandoned his responsibility?"

Culhane frowned. "The man's wife was home by herself. He wanted to get to her and protect her. There wasn't nothin' he could've done to protect the money at that point."

"Sorry," The Kid muttered. "I didn't mean for it to sound like that." If he had been able to save his wife, he would have turned his back on anything else in the world. "What happened?"

"When Reilly got there, they'd already set fire to the place, but he was able to get inside to try to get her out. He was too late. She was already dead. Shot in the head. From what the marshal at Fire Hill told me, Latch and his varmints started shootin' into houses as soon as they hit town, and Reilly's was one of the first places they came to. I reckon it's possible Miz Reilly was the first person in town they killed. But Reilly didn't know that until after he got inside the house. He tried to get her body out anyway, but the roof collapsed and trapped 'em both. Marshal Hyde barely got in there and dragged Reilly out before he burned up."

"Looks like he came pretty close to it anyway."

"Yeah. I didn't want him to come along. The local sawbones said he oughtn't even be out of bed, let alone ridin' with a posse. But Reilly's bound and determined to be there when we catch up to Latch. Says he's got a score to settle. I don't know about you, Morgan, but I can't argue with that."

"No." The Kid slowly shook his head and thought about his own quest for vengeance that had nearly consumed him. "I can't, either."

"I don't know if he's gonna make it. The doc gave him some pain medicine he keeps nippin' at, but even with that, he's got to be goin' through hell. I expect we'll wake up one mornin' and find him dead."

"I wouldn't be so sure about that," The Kid said as he looked at Vint Reilly pacing around impatiently. The need for revenge was a powerful motivating force, able to keep a man going long past the time when reason said he couldn't continue. He knew that from experience.

He looked back at Culhane. "You say there's a marshal at Fire Hill?"

"Yeah, Alonzo Hyde. He survived the fire and the shootin'."

"How come he didn't come along with the posse?"

"He would've, but he's an old man. Anyway, somebody had to stay there to see to the buryin' and protect what's left of the town. Folks will be goin' through the rubble tryin' to see if there's anything they can salvage. Maybe they'll try to

66

clear things off and rebuild. I don't know about that. Wouldn't surprise me none if everybody up and moved away and let what's left of the town go back to the earth. Might be the best thing."

The Kid thought that was right. Sometimes you could come back from a loss, but other times it was better to just let it all go. If he had died after avenging Rebel's murder, he wouldn't have counted it any great loss.

But he had managed to help quite a few people since then, he reminded himself. He supposed that was worth something.

"I'm going to hike back down there and get my horse and my pack animal," he told Culhane. "I'll be ready to ride by the time the rest of you are mounted."

The Ranger nodded. "Thanks for your help, Morgan. I'm glad you're ridin' with us. And again, I'm sorry about that little dustup earlier."

"Just ride herd on that posse of yours, Ranger. We don't want any more . . . little dustups."

By the time the horses were rounded up, The Kid had hiked down off the escarpment and whistled for the buckskin. The horse answered the call, and The Kid swung up into the saddle and rode after his pack horse.

The posse members picked their way down the slope, led by Culhane, and joined The Kid on the flats.

67

"Forty men can't help but leave a trail," Culhane said as they rode east by southeast.

The Kid wasn't any great shakes as a tracker, but even he could see the wide swath of hoof-prints they were following.

"And Latch don't really care if anybody comes after him," the Ranger went on. "Fella's arrogant as all get-out. Thinks he can do whatever he wants to and get away with it."

Ed Marchman, who was riding on Culhane's other side, grunted. "So far he's been right about that."

"The law will catch up to him sooner or later," Culhane responded. "That's one thing about the Rangers . . . we don't never give up."

"Sooner or later doesn't do us one damned bit of good," Marchman said. "It's already too late to save our town, and all of our people who were killed."

"Latch will answer for that," Culhane insisted.

Maybe, The Kid thought, but it wouldn't change anything. It was just something these men had to do in hopes of easing the pain inside them. Whether it would or not was pretty doubtful.

Of course, the punchers from the M-B Connected didn't have such a personal stake in it. Their homes hadn't been destroyed, and their loved ones hadn't been killed.

But the man they worked for had been stolen from, and if they were like most cowboys, they rode for the brand. That would be enough motive for them to go after Warren Latch.

The Kid looked at Vint Reilly and saw the way the stagecoach station manager was swaying in his saddle. Every so often Reilly slipped a small brown bottle from his saddlebags and took a tiny swig from it.

That would be the pain medicine Culhane had mentioned, The Kid thought. Laudanum, more than likely. He was surprised Reilly wasn't passed out in a drugged stupor.

Reilly was taking just enough medicine to make the pain bearable, but not enough to blunt it too much. He embraced the pain, relying on it to keep him awake and alert. To keep him going, along with his need for vengeance.

The kindest thing anybody could do for him might be to draw a gun and put a bullet through his head, The Kid mused.

But every man had the right to choose his own hell.

The Kid's horse drifted away from Culhane's mount. He didn't realize he was riding next to Nick Burton until the young man said, "Mr. Morgan, isn't it?"

The Kid looked over at him and nodded. "That's right."

"Are you the one they call Kid Morgan?"

The Kid's eyes narrowed in surprise. "How'd you know that?"

He spoke quietly, hoping Nick would keep his voice down.

"I've read about you. In the dime novels."

The Kid smiled. When Conrad Browning had been casting about for a new identity to conceal the fact that he was still alive and on the trail of his wife's murderers, he had come up with Kid Morgan, basing his appearance and actions on the sort of characters he had read about in those lurid, yellow-backed tales.

Most people didn't want to admit they had never heard of Kid Morgan, so to make themselves sound savvy, they pretended to know all about him and helped spread the deception when they gossiped about him.

Somewhere along the way, the carefully cultivated fiction had become fact. Conrad had settled into his life as Kid Morgan and preferred to live that way now. The few times he had adopted the identity of Conrad Browning again had not worked out well.

In an odd way, his life imitating art had become art imitating life, if you could call such fantastical scribblings as the dime novels art. In the past year or so, books featuring the totally made-up exploits of one Kid Morgan, Gunfighter, had begun to appear, published by companies back east.

The same thing had happened to his father, back when Frank Morgan first began to acquire a reputation as a fast gun. The Kid wasn't completely surprised it was happening again.

Nick was digging around in his saddlebags. "I brought one with me, but I haven't had a chance to start reading it yet." He pulled out a slim volume with a yellow cover, not much bigger than a pamphlet, and held it out toward The Kid. "Here."

The Kid took it, his eyebrows lifting as he read the title on the cheaply printed book, *Kid Morgan and The Drifter, or, Brothers on the Trail.* As he rocked along in the saddle, he opened the book and skimmed through the pages of densely packed type. "This is about me and Frank Morgan."

"Yeah," Nick agreed eagerly. "I never knew you and The Drifter were brothers."

The Kid laughed and handed the dime novel back to the youngster. "That's because we're not. I hate to disappoint you, Nick, but Frank Morgan is definitely not my brother."

"Oh. You mean they made it all up?"

"That's what they do."

"But have you ever *met* The Drifter?"

"Our trails have crossed a few times," The Kid evaded. "He's quite a bit older than me."

"Is he as fast as everybody says he is?"

The Kid gave him an honest answer. "Yeah. He's the fastest I've ever seen."

"Faster than you?"

"Faster than me." The Kid nodded, adding, "But not by much."

"And I get to ride with you and fight outlaws with you," Nick said. "The fellas back at the boarding school in Philadelphia would never believe this."

Obviously, the young man had a bad case of hero worship, The Kid thought. That wasn't good. It could prove to be a distraction, and where they were, getting distracted at the wrong moment could get somebody killed in a hurry.

"Why don't you put that up," The Kid suggested, "and if it's all right with you, we'll just keep this between ourselves."

"You don't want the rest of the posse to know who you really are?"

"I'd just as soon they didn't."

Nick thought about it, nodded, and slipped the dime novel back in his saddlebag. "All right, Kid . . . I mean, Mr. Morgan. We'll just leave it at that."

"I'm obliged to you."

"But when I get back to the ranch, will it be all right if I send letters to some of my friends from school and tell them about this?"

The Kid laughed. "I don't see why not."

That was assuming Nick made it back to his grandfather's ranch alive, The Kid thought as he grew more solemn.

From what he had heard about the men they were chasing, it was possible none of them would make it out of this pursuit alive.

CHAPTER 9

Slim Duval was sitting with his back against a rock, sipping from the silver flask in his hand, when Latch came up and tapped the toe of his boot against Duval's foot.

"Get up," Latch said. "We have things to do."

"What?" Duval looked around. The gang had made camp and eaten supper, and he was ready to get some sleep after spending another long day in the saddle. "I thought we were done for the day."

"You thought wrong. Now get up."

Duval shrugged, screwed the cap on the flask, and slipped it into an inner coat pocket. He pushed himself to his feet.

As the member of the gang who had been with Latch the longest and also as the second-in-command, he was the only one of the outlaws who could get away with failing to follow an order from Latch instantly and without question. Anybody else would be subject to a reprimand that was always painful and occasionally fatal.

Duval was the closest thing Latch had to a friend, however, so he cut him some slack. As they headed for the horses, Duval asked, "Where are we going?"

"I don't know. I just feel drawn to take a ride. I think there's something waiting out there for us."

Duval had experience with Latch's hunches. It was another part of the man's crazed personality, claiming he sometimes heard voices speaking to him from out of nowhere, telling him what to do.

"One of those ghosts been talking to you again?" Duval asked.

It was a mistake. Latch stopped short and turned sharply toward him. "Don't you say anything about that. I know what I hear, damn you!"

"Sorry, boss," Duval said quickly. "I didn't mean anything by it. You know I believe those voices are there."

"Of course they are. I'm not crazy enough to imagine things like that."

That was where he was wrong, Duval thought. Warren Latch was plenty loco enough to imagine such things.

But Slim Duval was way too smart to express that opinion where Latch could hear it.

As he started toward the horses again with his long duster swinging around his legs, Latch went on, " As a matter of fact, no one has told me to take a ride tonight. It's just a feeling on my part. It may be somebody trying to communicate with me, but if that's the case, I can't see or hear them."

"So it's a hunch," Duval said. "I'm fine with that, Warren. Nobody has better hunches than you do."

"You'd do well to remember that," Latch snapped.

"I'm not likely to forget it."

They saddled their horses, Latch throwing his own hull on his mount. He wasn't one to pawn off a chore onto anybody else when he could do it himself.

A burly Mexican named Ortiz wandered over to them. He frowned at the horses they were getting ready to ride.

"We are going somewhere, *jefe*?" he asked Latch.

"Slim and I are going to do some scouting," Latch said. "The rest of you will stay here. Post guards as usual. We'll be back later."

"*Sí, señor.*"

The two men swung up into their saddles and rode off into the night. Duval let Latch take the lead, thinking it was possible they might just ride around aimlessly for a while and then return to camp.

Either that, or Latch's instincts would actually lead them to something.

When they had gone a short distance, Duval asked, "Doesn't it worry you, leaving that bunch of robbers and cutthroats back there with the loot from our last three jobs? What if they decide to move the camp and take all the money with them?"

"They won't do that," Latch said with supreme confidence. "They know if they did, I would hunt them down and kill them all, even if I had to follow them to the ends of the earth."

Duval didn't doubt it for a second. And Latch was right. The rest of the men knew that, too.

"Another week and we'll be in San Antonio," Duval mused.

It was where they always went when they had accumulated enough loot. The city was large enough a group of men could get lost in the population, especially if they didn't ride in together. The gang would stop outside town and divvy up the money, then scatter in twos and threes, or sometimes just a single man, to enter the city inconspicuously.

Duval looked forward to playing poker at the Buckhorn and the other saloons downtown and visiting the warm, brown-skinned señoritas in the brothels.

Of course, in San Antonio, a man with money could have any sort of woman he wanted, from blond Scandanavians to ebony-tressed Chinese to dusky Africans. Duval had sampled the charms of all of them in his time.

As for what Latch did while he was in San Antone, Duval had no idea. The man always disappeared with no explanation of where he could be found.

Weeks would go by, weeks spent in idle dissipation by the Cajun gambler, and then one day Latch would be there, finding him in some unknown manner and saying it was time for them to ride again. The word would go out to the other members of the gang, and they would rendezvous at a place Latch selected, then set out on another long raid.

"Let slip the dogs of war," Duval thought, recalling that quote from something he had heard somewhere. Maybe not war in the commonly accepted sense of nation against nation, but it was safe to say Warren Latch was at war with the whole world. And Duval and the other members of the gang were his dog soldiers.

Those were fine thoughts for a dark night, he told himself as he shook them out of his head.

Anyway, it wasn't a completely dark night, he suddenly realized. A dim yellow light was burning several hundred yards in front of them.

Damned if Latch's hunch hadn't led them to something, after all.

"Is that where we're going?" Duval asked quietly.

"I want to see what's there," Latch replied.

As they rode closer, a dog began to bark. Latch reined in, and Duval followed suit. Their eyes, well adjusted to the darkness, could make out a double cabin with a covered dogtrot in between. Beyond it lay a barn and a corral, along with a couple sheds. This was a small ranch of some sort, far from the nearest town.

"Chances are these folks won't have much money, Warren," Duval said. "I don't know if they'd be worth bothering with—"

At that moment, a door in one side of the cabin

opened, letting out more light. A figure stepped into the doorway, foolishly silhouetted against the glow of a lamp in the room.

"Tip, what are you barking at?" a woman's voice called. "What's out there?"

Her voice was clear and sounded relatively young to Duval. He squinted and was able to make out the shape of her as she stood in the doorway. It was an appealing shape.

He could also see that she was holding something. A rifle, by the look of it.

"A woman," Latch breathed.

"Yeah, a woman with a gun," Duval said.

"She must be alone here. If there was a man, he would have come to the door to speak to the dog instead of her."

That made sense to Duval, but he still didn't see any point in bothering this woman when in less than a week they would be in San Antonio and could have all the whores they wanted.

He didn't recall Latch ever expressing much interest in women. Duval didn't know what the man did between raids, but he'd always assumed Latch was the kind of madman who preferred killing to loving.

"If it was me, I think I'd ride on back to camp and forget about this place, boss," Duval said, knowing Latch wouldn't kill him out of hand for offering a piece of advice like that. "But I'll do whatever you say, of course."

"I say we take a closer look," Latch declared. He gigged his horse forward.

Duval managed not to sigh as he followed.

The dog was still barking. The woman called him to her, gripped him by the scruff of the neck, and took him inside. The door closed, cutting off the light. The yellow glow still showed in the window.

When they were about fifty yards from the cabin, Latch and Duval dismounted, moving forward on foot. Latch drew one of his Mausers, and Duval followed suit with his Colt.

The window was open to allow fresh air into the cabin on the warm night . . . and it let the aroma of fresh-baked bread out into the darkness, as well. The smell made Duval's mouth water.

Close enough to hear voices, the outlaws heard the woman say, "Paula, when you and Helen finish with the dishes you can go on to bed."

Another female voice replied, "But I thought you wanted me to tend to the horses, Mama."

"Which you should have done before it got dark," the older woman said. "I'll do it. I just want to give whatever stirred up old Tip a few minutes to drift on its way."

"What do you reckon it was, Mama?" That was a third slightly different female voice.

Three women, Duval thought as his heart started to pound a little harder in spite of himself. And apparently they were alone.

"Might have been a wolf or a panther," the mother replied. "More than likely, though, it was just a coyote."

"Or an Indian," one of the daughters suggested.

"Hush, girl," the mother said. "There's not a savage within a hundred miles of here, and you know it."

Well now, she was wrong about that, mused Duval.

Warren Latch's skin might be white instead of red, but Latch was as savage as any Comanche or Apache who had ever roamed the plains. Maybe more so.

The two of them flanked the window, moving with the stealth of true predators. Duval edged an eye over the edge to risk a look.

Gauzy curtains hung on the inside of the window, but they didn't prevent him from seeing the woman sitting at a table petting the black-and-white dog at her feet. She was in her late thirties, he guessed, and still attractive, with honey-colored hair that hung past her shoulders.

On the other side of the room, two girls worked at a washtub, one of them rinsing dishes while the other dried them with a cloth. They were seventeen or eighteen, Duval judged. Their hair was fairer than their mother's, and they wore it braided. As their heads turned so he could see their identical features, he realized they were twins.

Son . . . of . . . a . . . *bitch,* Duval thought. Twins.

"Tip's calmed down now. I'll go on out to the barn." The woman stood up. "Come on, boy."

As the big, shaggy dog got to its feet to follow her, Duval realized the animal was old and made its way with a halting gait. It might not be able to see or hear very well, either, but it could probably smell him and Latch.

Thinking the same thing, Latch jerked his head for Duval to follow him and retreated around the corner of the cabin.

"We'll follow the woman and take her prisoner," Latch whispered. "With her as our captive, those girls will be much easier to handle. They'll do whatever we say. Once we have them all under control, you can ride back to camp and fetch the rest of the men. We'll spend the night here."

Duval was a little disappointed he and Latch weren't going to keep the women for themselves, but Latch was nothing if not loyal to his men. That made them loyal to him, despite him being loco.

"All right, boss," Duval breathed.

The woman stepped out of the cabin and started toward the barn with the old dog trailing slowly behind her. She was carrying the rifle again.

"Wait until she gets in the barn," Latch ordered. "I'll grab the woman, you kill the dog."

Duval nodded. They waited until the woman

disappeared into the barn. A faint glow appeared through the open door. The woman had lit a lantern.

Silently, the two men approached the structure. They moved into the entrance.

The woman had leaned the rifle, an old Henry, against one of the stalls and had a pitchfork in her hands as she forked some fresh hay into the stalls for several horses quartered there.

The dog suddenly turned toward the men and growled. Latch rushed forward. Duval drew his gun as he lunged through the door. The animal tried to bite him but was too slow. Duval's gun rose and fell, thudding against the animal's head and causing it to collapse on the barn's hard-packed dirt floor.

He could have hit the dog again and made sure it was dead, but he didn't bother. The old critter was no real threat.

Meanwhile, the woman didn't scream when she saw the two men charging into the barn. Her face grim, she counterattacked, thrusting the sharp tines of the pitchfork at Latch.

He twisted aside, but the fork ripped a hole in his duster. It hung on the coat for a second, long enough for him to grab the handle and twist the pitchfork out of the woman's grip. He spun it around and cracked the handle against her head. With a groan, she fell to her knees.

Duval's eyes widened in surprise as Latch

reversed the pitchfork again and drove the tines deep into the woman's chest.

She gasped in shock and pain and pawed feebly at the pitchfork. Latch ripped it out of her body. Blood started to well from the five holes it left behind. The woman's eyes rolled up in her head, and she fell forward on her face.

"You killed her," Duval said into the hush that fell over the barn. The horses were moving around in the stalls, spooked by the violence and the smell of blood.

"She tried to kill me," Latch said as if that were the only explanation needed. "You can still tell those girls that she's our prisoner out here. That will do nicely. Go and get them."

With Latch standing there holding a pitchfork with blood still dripping from its tines, Duval wasn't about to argue with him. He nodded. "Sure."

In truth, he was glad to get out of the barn. The way Latch had killed the woman, swiftly, coldly, and emotionlessly, had spooked him, too.

As he approached the cabin, gun in hand again, he heard the young women talking. One of them was saying, "—be glad when Pa and the boys get back tomorrow."

"I will be, too," the other one agreed.

Duval stepped into the doorway and leveled his Colt. "Sorry, ladies. Somebody else is coming to call first."

CHAPTER 10

Nick Burton kept his word that night when the posse made camp. He didn't say anything about who the newest member of the group really was . . . at least as far as The Kid could tell.

He felt confident if Nick *had* said something about his reputation as a gunfighter, at least some of the men would be looking at him from the corners of their eyes and whispering. Instead, most of them ignored him.

The Kid had his own supplies, so he fixed his own supper, although he used the common campfire to do it. While he was sitting on a rock eating the beans and bacon he had warmed up, Culhane came over to him and sat down, too.

"You willin' to take a turn standin' guard tonight?" the Ranger asked.

"Sure," The Kid replied without hesitation. "If I'm going to ride with you, I'll do my part."

"Figured as much." Culhane had brought a cup of coffee with him and took a sip.

"How are the wounded men doing?"

In addition to the man with the bullet hole in his arm, another posse man had been creased in the side.

"They'll live," Culhane said. "I'd send Gordon back—he's the one who got the crease and lost quite a bit of blood—if I didn't need every man I got."

"He can't be in as bad a shape as Reilly."

Culhane drank some more coffee and said quietly, "Ain't that the truth."

Reilly was on the other side of camp, sitting cross-legged on the ground. He was slumped over, and his head sagged forward on his chest.

"Is he asleep?" The Kid asked with a frown.

"Could be," Culhane said. "He's burned all over. Can't stretch out to sleep without it hurtin' him too bad, he says. Next settlement we come to, I'm leavin' him there, even if I have to hog-tie him to do it."

"He won't like that."

"I don't care. I can't stand to watch what he's doin' to himself anymore."

Culhane was in charge of the posse, so it was his decision to make, but The Kid figured Reilly would put up a fight. In the end, though, Culhane would probably get his way.

"What guard shift do you want me to take?"

"Get some sleep while you can," Culhane said. "I'll wake you up after a while."

The Kid nodded his agreement. He had already tended to his horses, so as soon as he finished his supper and used sand to clean the pan, he spread his bedroll and stretched out. The Kid did his watch and all was quiet.

The dry air lost the day's heat rapidly at night,

and it was pleasantly cool the next morning in the pre-dawn hours as the posse ate breakfast and got ready to ride.

It wouldn't stay that way very long, The Kid thought as a breeze stirred the air. Once the sun was up, the temperature would begin to climb. When the posse moved out, The Kid rode next to Culhane again. None of the others questioned his right to be there.

"What's in this direction?" The Kid asked.

Grinning, Culhane replied, "Well, San Antonio, if you keep goin' far enough. But it's five or six days' ride away from here, at least. In between there are a few little towns and some ranches and a whole lot of nothin'. You ever been to Texas before, Morgan?"

"Yeah, but not this part. I've been to San Antonio, though. Do you think that's where Latch is headed?"

The Ranger rubbed his jaw as he pondered the question. "Could be. Plenty of folks in San Antone. Latch and his men might be able to blend in there. Every time after they've pulled a few jobs, they drop out of sight for a while, so we know they're goin' somewhere and hidin' out."

As the morning went on, the posse rode through more of those miles of nothing Culhane had mentioned. The Kid heard muttering from some of the men, so when they paused to rest the horses, he caught a moment alone with

86

Culhane. "How far are these men willing to go?"

"I thought you said you hadn't ridden with a posse before."

"I haven't."

Culhane chuckled. "Maybe not, but you seem to know that once fellas have been gone from home for a few days, they start wantin' to turn around and go back." The lawman grew serious. "With this bunch, though, the ones from Fire Hill don't have any homes to go back to. Most of 'em are single men, so they don't have families to worry about, either. And old man Burton ordered his punchers not to come back without his money, so they ain't gonna be inclined to give up." Culhane nodded. "I think they'll all stick, at least for a while longer."

"I hope you're right," The Kid said.

They pushed on.

After a while Nick Burton moved his horse up alongside The Kid's buckskin. "How are you today, Mr. Morgan?"

"I'm fine, Nick. How about you?"

"All right, I guess." Nick shifted in the saddle. "This is the most I've ever ridden, though. I'm a mite sore."

"Did you grow up on your grandfather's ranch?"

"No, sir. We lived in Dallas. My father's a businessman. Has a furniture store there. It's very successful."

"Successful enough that he sent you to school in Philadelphia, I guess."

"That's right. I've spent the past few summers on the M-B Connected, though. My grandpa insisted on it." Nick hesitated. "I think he has some idea that I'm going to take over the ranch someday."

"How do you feel about that?" The Kid asked. The conversation helped pass the time.

"I'd love to," Nick replied eagerly. "To tell you the truth, Mr. Morgan, I've never been that fond of the idea of selling furniture the rest of my life."

The Kid had to laugh. "To tell you the truth, I don't think I'd be happy about that, either."

Not after all the changes he had gone through. Business just didn't have any appeal for him anymore, although there had been a time in his life when he had practically lived for the thrill of dealing in high finance.

"I don't know if I'm up to running the ranch, though," Nick said. "You may have noticed, I'm not very big."

"What does that matter? If you're in charge, and you let everybody else know that you're in charge, folks tend to forget about how tall you are . . . or aren't."

"I'd like to think you're right, but I've never been the sort to take over at anything."

"Maybe you'll grow into it."

"Maybe," Nick said with a doubtful shrug. "Did

you grow into being what you are, Mr. Morgan?"

"I guess you could say that," The Kid replied.

But it was more like fate had thrust his current life upon him, and a cruel fate, at that. He had come through the fires of tragedy and loss, and for a time he had found hope again.

Then that hope had been snatched away from him, too, leaving him to drift aimlessly. As far as he could see into the future at this moment, that was going to be his life.

Culhane called, "Everybody hold it!"

The Kid reined in, as did the other members of the posse. Culhane sat up straight in his saddle, craned his neck, and peered into the distance.

"Looks like a little ranch house yonder," he announced. "We'll noon there and water the horses. Before we do, I reckon somebody ought to ride up there and scout the place. Latch has tried to spring one trap on us already. We ain't gonna waltz right into another one with our eyes closed."

The Ranger turned his head to look at The Kid. "How about you and young Burton there check it out, Morgan?"

The Kid nodded, but Nick gulped. "Me? You want me to scout the place, Ranger Culhane?"

"That's what I just said, ain't it?"

"I don't know if I can—"

"It'll be all right, Nick," The Kid interrupted him. "We can handle it."

Nick took a deep breath. "Well, if you say so."

89

But he didn't sound convinced that it was a good idea.

"If it's all clear, give us a high sign and we'll come on in," Culhane told The Kid as he and Nick rode past the Ranger.

The Kid nodded. He and Nick left the posse behind and rode toward the ranch house, which sat on the plains about a mile ahead of them.

After a minute, Nick said, "I don't know if Ranger Culhane should've picked me for this job, but I've got to admit, it's pretty exciting being on a scouting mission with the famous Kid Morgan."

"Get your Winchester out," The Kid advised as he pulled his own rifle from the saddle boot, not commenting on Nick's assessment of his fame. "You see that barn?"

"Yeah. What about it?"

"Keep your eyes on it," The Kid told him. "Do you see anybody moving around?"

"No. There are three or four horses in the corral, though."

"Watch the barn. If you see sunlight reflect off anything, you let me know right away, understand?"

"Sure. Are you watching the house for the same thing, Mr. Morgan?"

"That's right," The Kid said. "If there's a chance of a trap and you see the sun glinting on something, it's likely to be a gun. If it's not, if it turns out to be something harmless, you haven't lost anything by being careful."

"I'll remember that." Nick paused for a second, then added with youthful enthusiasm, "I wish I could ride with you all the time, Mr. Morgan!"

"No," The Kid said flatly. "You don't."

In reality, he was probably only five or six years older than Nick Burton. But at this moment, he felt at least a hundred years older than the youngster.

The Kid didn't see any signs of trouble waiting for them at the ranch, but he didn't see any signs of life, either, except the horses in the corral. That was a little troubling.

People should have been moving around, going about the day's work. If not for the horses, he would have begun to wonder if the ranch had been abandoned.

When they were about two hundred yards from the buildings, The Kid signaled for Nick to stop. They reined in and dismounted, taking their rifles with them.

"We'll leave the horses here and go ahead on foot," The Kid said. "Keep your eyes open. Don't shoot at anything unless you're absolutely sure what it is you're shooting at."

The last thing they needed was for Nick to gun down some unsuspecting rancher, The Kid thought.

Silently, he motioned Nick toward the barn as

they approached. The Kid closed in on the house. The double cabin had chimneys at both ends, but smoke wasn't coming from either of them.

At this time of day, somebody should have been preparing a midday meal. The fact that they weren't was a bad sign.

The Kid looked at the dogtrot and frowned. No dog had bounded out and started barking at them as they approached.

Of course, just because the cabin was designed with that open area between its two halves didn't mean the family had to have a dog. That was just what it was called.

However, nearly every ranch had at least one big cur on it, and no barking had greeted the newcomers. In fact, an eerie silence hung over the place. Every nerve in The Kid's body told him something was badly wrong.

Quietly, he moved into the shade under the dogtrot. The door of the cabin to his left was closed, but the one on the right stood open.

"Anybody home?" he called.

There was no answer.

The Kid glanced toward the barn. One of the big double doors was partially open, and as he watched, Nick disappeared through that dark gap.

The Kid stepped to the open door of the cabin and looked inside. The first thing he saw was an overturned chair, and beyond it on the floor a couple broken dishes.

A fight of some sort had taken place in there, but no one was inside now.

He moved back into the dogtrot and turned toward the barn. As he did, Nick suddenly let out a startled yell and came into sight again, backing up as fast as he could, practically running backward, in fact.

He tried to point his rifle at the barn, but as he lifted the weapon he got his feet tangled up and went over backward, sitting down so hard dust puffed up around him. He grunted from the impact and dropped the Winchester.

A man stepped out of the barn holding a revolver. "I don't know who you are, boy, but you poked your nose into the wrong place!"

The gun came up, and The Kid knew Nick was only instants away from having the life blasted out of him.

CHAPTER 11

That was plenty of time for The Kid to react.

The Winchester snapped to his shoulder. With a round already in the chamber, all he had to do was settle the sights on the gunman's forehead and squeeze the trigger.

The whipcrack of the shot filled the air.

The man's head jerked back as the bullet smashed into his forehead, bored through his brain, and exploded out the back of his head in a grisly pink spray of blood, gray matter, and bone shards. His knees came unhinged, dropping him straight to the ground. The pistol fell from his limp fingers, unfired.

"Move, Nick!" The Kid shouted. He didn't know if there were any more would-be killers lurking inside the barn, but if there were, he wanted the youngster out of the line of fire.

Nick rolled onto hands and knees and scrambled to his feet. As he did, shots erupted from inside the barn.

Plumes of dust geysered into the air around Nick's feet as he ran toward the barn's far corner. The Kid slammed three fast shots through the open door of the barn and then ran across the space between it and the house, angling for the nearest corner of the barn. There might be another way in around back.

From the sound of the shots, probably two or three men were inside, he guessed. He and Nick were outnumbered, but only for the moment. The shooting would bring Culhane and the rest of the posse in a hurry.

The Kid saw Nick vanish around the other corner of the barn. From the way the young man was moving so quickly, he wasn't hurt. That was pure luck . . . luck, and Kid Morgan's fast reflexes and deadly aim.

The Kid ducked through the bars of the corral

and trotted along the side of the barn. When he reached the rear corner, he peered around it.

There was a door back there, all right, big enough for a man to lead a horse out through it.

The corral extended around to the back of the barn as well, forming an L-shape around the building. The horses, spooked by the shooting in front, had all retreated back there and were milling around nervously.

The rear door burst open and three men rushed out, obviously intent on getting to their horses and fleeing. From the corner, The Kid opened fire, cutting down one man. He had to pull back when the two still on their feet started blazing away at him with six-guns as they ran.

"Hyaaah!"

That shout came from Nick, The Kid realized. What in blazes was he doing?

Hoofbeats pounded. The Kid risked a look. Nick had climbed into the corral from the other corner and was driving the startled horses toward the gunmen by running at them, shouting, and waving his hat.

One of the men twisted and fired at Nick. Clouds of dust had started to billow and swirl in the air, and The Kid couldn't see if Nick was hit.

A bullet from the other man's gun sizzled past his ear. He fired the Winchester again and saw the man double over as the slug punched into his guts.

The last man yelled in alarm as he tried to get out of the way of a running horse. The animal clipped him with a shoulder anyway, and the impact knocked the man off his feet.

He dropped his gun when he hit the ground. Scrambling after it, he'd just picked it up when Nick came out of the dust, his own revolver clutched in both hands.

It was a double-action weapon, and Nick fired it again and again as fast as he could pull the trigger, as the bullets pounded down into the outlaw on the ground.

Nick didn't stop jerking the trigger until the hammer clicked on an empty chamber. Even then he tried to shoot a couple more times before he realized he was out of bullets.

"Take it easy, Nick," The Kid said in a steadying voice as he walked up. "It's over."

Tears ran down the young man's face, cutting wet trails in the dust that coated his features.

"I . . . I killed him."

"You sure did," The Kid said. "I've got a hunch he had it coming."

"If you saw . . . if you saw what I did inside . . ."

Nick dropped the empty gun, fell to his knees, then curled up on his side and sobbed.

Quickly, The Kid checked the three men on the ground to make sure they were dead. Satisfied that they were, he stepped through the rear door into the barn.

It smelled like a typical barn full of hay and manure, but underlying those familiar scents was something else, something grim, a coppery smell The Kid recognized . . . and wished he didn't.

Freshly spilled blood. A lot of it.

His eyes adjusted quickly to the dimness inside the barn. It didn't take him long to find the nude bodies of two young women.

Little more than girls, really, they would never grow any older. Both were dead, butchered savagely. They had been beaten, probably assaulted repeatedly, and their throats were cut. Even with their faces twisted by agony, The Kid could tell they were twins.

Yeah, the bastard that Nick had shot to doll rags had had it coming, all right, and so had his three companions. The Kid knew Nick would probably be haunted by nightmares over what he had seen, but hoped the youngster never lost a second's sleep over exterminating vermin like that.

A new sound caught The Kid's attention. He turned and brought up the rifle as a growl came from a shadowy stall on the other side of the barn. Carefully, he moved toward it.

When he could see into the stall, he made out the body of another woman lying on a pile of hay. The front of her dress was dark with a huge, dried bloodstain. It looked like she had been shot or stabbed in several places.

A large, shaggy black-and-white dog sat at her

feet, snarling and growling at The Kid. The dog didn't make any move to get up and attack him. It stayed planted right where it was, protecting the body of its mistress.

"It's all right, fella," The Kid said. "I won't hurt you. I didn't do this."

The dog couldn't understand the words, but The Kid's calm tone seemed to get through to it. Moving awkwardly, it lay down and rested its head on its paws.

Hoofbeats thundered up outside. The rest of the posse had arrived.

"Morgan!" Culhane shouted. "Morgan, where are you?"

The Kid walked to the front of the barn and pulled the partially open door back farther. He stepped out, and looked up at the Ranger and his men. "I hope you brought some shovels with you, Culhane. You've got some burying to do."

Culhane insisted they bury the four dead outlaws, too.

"I ain't gonna just leave 'em here to either rot or get drug off by scavengers," the Ranger said. "We'll put 'em in the ground . . . but I damn sure ain't sayin' any words over 'em. Wouldn't make any difference, anyway. I reckon the Devil's already got 'em."

All four of the outlaws were dumped in a shallow mass grave. With the women it was different. The posse members all pitched in and dug three deep graves for them. Culhane found blankets in the house in which to wrap the bodies.

"I wish we could take the time to nail together some coffins for these poor ladies," he said as he stepped back from the shrouded shapes. "But we got to get back on the trail of the sons o' bitches who did this."

"You think Latch and his men are responsible for what happened here?" The Kid asked.

"You saw the tracks yourself," Culhane said. "A big bunch rode up here and then rode out again in the last twelve hours. It's got to be them."

"And those men were part of the gang?" The Kid nodded toward the mass grave.

"Bound to be."

"Why did Latch leave them behind?"

Culhane shook his head. "I don't know. Don't reckon it really matters, either."

He was right about that, The Kid supposed.

When the bodies had been lowered gently into the graves and the holes refilled, the members of the posse gathered around and took off their hats. The old dog sat at the foot of the graves, whining softly as if he knew what was going on.

"I'll say somethin'," Culhane said, "unless somebody else wants to."

No one volunteered, so after a moment the Ranger began to pray. He asked for mercy on the souls of the three women, and justice for the evil men who had harmed them. The prayer was short and simple, and when it was over several of the men muttered, "Amen."

As they put their hats on and started to turn away, Nick Burton spoke up. "What about the dog?"

The sound of a shot startled everyone. The old dog crashed to the ground, shot through the head.

A few feet away, Vint Reilly stood with his revolver in his bandaged hand. A tendril of smoke curled from the barrel.

The Kid heard a terrible cry but didn't realize it was coming from his own throat. He wasn't aware that he was moving, either, until he had batted the gun out of Reilly's hand, grabbed the front of the burned man's shirt, and started shaking him.

"You bastard!" The Kid roared at Reilly. "What did you do that for?"

"Morgan!" Culhane yelled. "Morgan, stop it! Somebody grab him, damn it!"

Reilly wasn't putting up a fight. He just stood there, his head jerking back and forth as The Kid shook him.

A second later, a couple men grabbed The Kid's arms behind him and dragged him away from Reilly, who didn't show any more reaction to being rescued than he had to being attacked.

The Kid stood there panting with anger as the

men hung on to him. Reilly bent down slowly and picked up the gun The Kid had knocked out of his hand.

Culhane had his Colt out, pointed in Reilly's general direction. "You'd better holster that hog-leg, mister."

Reilly calmly replaced the bullet he had fired, then slid the gun back into leather.

"And you'd better have a good explanation of why you did that," Culhane added.

"It was a kindness," Reilly rasped, forcing the words from his smoke-tortured throat.

"A kindness?" Culhane repeated. "How in blazes do you figure that?"

"You saw . . . how old and crippled . . . that dog was. What were you going to do? Leave him here . . . to starve?"

"You didn't have to kill him," Nick said. "We could have taken him with us."

"He never could have . . . kept up."

As much as The Kid hated to admit it, Reilly had a point about that, he thought as the red haze of rage that had fallen over his brain began to recede. But the callousness of the man's action still bothered him.

"Besides," Reilly went on, "everything the dog loved . . . was dead. What reason did it have . . . to go on living?"

Several members of the posse turned to look away uncomfortably, obviously thinking the same thing that went through the mind of everyone there.

Reilly was in pretty much the same shape as that dog, wasn't he?

And hadn't The Kid thought just the day before that the kindest thing anybody could do for the man was to put a bullet through his head?

"Let me go," The Kid said quietly to the men holding him. "I'm all right now."

Culhane nodded for the men to release him. As they did so, one of the cowboys from the M-B Connected suddenly said, "Riders coming fast!"

Everyone turned and saw three men on horse-back galloping toward the ranch. Men riding that fast usually meant trouble, and this time was no exception. A second later a bullet whistled overhead, followed instantly by the sharp crack of a shot.

Chapter 12

"Take cover!" Culhane bellowed. The posse members hotfooted it for the barn, which was the closest structure.

The three riders continued to shoot. Firing from the backs of running horses at a distance of a couple hundred yards made their bullets go wild. As far as The Kid could tell, all the posse men reached cover without being hit.

He found himself just inside the barn door with Culhane. The Ranger peered out. "It takes men who are powerful foolish—or powerful mad—to charge a force that's got 'em outnumbered eight to one."

"You think they're some of Latch's men?" The Kid asked.

"I reckon it's more likely they've got some connection with this ranch. The menfolks who live here, maybe."

"Is that the reason you ordered everybody to take cover instead of shooting back at them?"

Culhane nodded. "I ain't gonna make things worse here by killin' somebody who's got every right in the world to be mad." He turned his head and called, "Everybody hold your fire. No shootin' unless I give the word."

The Kid hoped the members of the posse followed that order better than they had the day before, when Clyde Fenner and the others had opened fire on him as soon as they spotted him.

The shooting stopped, and The Kid couldn't hear hoofbeats anymore. The three riders must have reached the graves.

Culhane seemed to have drawn the same conclusion. "I'm goin' out there. Somebody needs to talk to those fellas and find out just what's goin' on here."

"Not by yourself," The Kid said. "I'm coming with you."

"I ain't askin' for volunteers."

"Didn't say you were."

Culhane shrugged and nodded. His gun was already in his hand as he said, "All right, come on." He raised his voice. "The rest of you stay here."

"What if they kill you, Culhane?" Ed Marchman asked from where he crouched behind the wall of a stall. "What are we supposed to do then?"

"I reckon that'll be up to you. If it was up to me, though, I'd be careful not to get any innocent blood on my hands."

"Anybody who shoots down a Texas Ranger isn't innocent," Marchman snapped.

"You got a point," Culhane agreed, "but I still say don't get trigger-happy." With that, he stepped out into the open.

The Kid was at his side, Colt also drawn.

They moved carefully to the corner of the barn, and as they did, they heard sobbing.

When they reached a spot where they could see the three graves where the women were laid to rest, they stopped. One of the men had thrown himself on the ground at the foot of the graves, next to the body of the dog. The other two stood protectively over him, rifles raised.

"Hey, you fellas!" Culhane called. "Don't shoot! We need to talk to you."

The two men with rifles snapped the weapons up and pointed them toward the barn.

They were young, probably in their early twenties, The Kid saw at a glimpse before he and Culhane pulled back. Both were blond, with a definite resemblance not only between them but also to the two young women who had fallen victim to the outlaws. The Kid figured they were brothers to those two sisters.

He had already pegged the older woman for their mother, so that meant the man sobbing wretchedly over the graves was probably her husband and the father of the twins, as well as the two young men who had ridden up with him.

"Hold your fire," Culhane went on. "We didn't do this. I give you my word on that. I'm a Texas Ranger, name of Asa Culhane, and I wouldn't lie to you."

"How do we know that?" one of the young men asked.

"If you'll let me step out where you can see me without shootin' me, you'll see the badge on my shirt," Culhane said.

A moment of silence passed, broken only by the continued crying.

Finally, the one who had spoken said, "All right, come on. But you'd better have empty hands, mister."

"That's fine." Culhane holstered his Colt. He glanced back at his companion. "Stay here, Morgan."

The Kid nodded. Culhane lifted his hands so

they would be in plain sight and stepped away from the barn, moving so the men at the graves could see him.

It took a lot of guts to step into the sights of two rifles like that, The Kid thought. But courage was something Texas Rangers had never been short on, according to everything he'd heard.

The two young men spoke quickly and quietly to each other. The Kid couldn't make out the words. Then one of them asked, "You're really a Ranger, mister?"

"I am," Culhane said. "I'm leading a posse after a gang of owlhoots. We figure they're the ones who . . . did this."

The young man's voice broke a little as he asked, "What . . . what did you find here?"

"Three women," Culhane said, making his voice as gentle as he could. "One older lady and two gals who looked like twins."

"Oh, Lord . . . I thought maybe . . . we hoped . . ."

"But we knew all along it had to be them," the other one said, "as soon as we saw the graves."

"I'm sorry, boys," Culhane said. "I can't tell you how sorry we all are."

He glanced over at The Kid and moved his head, indicating The Kid should come out from the cover of the barn wall. The Kid did so, but only after holstering his gun.

"This here is Morgan, another fella from the

posse," Culhane went on. "He can tell you more about it than I can. Him and another fella ridin' with us caught some of the varmints who did this."

The Ranger pointed at the mound of dirt that marked the mass grave. "That's the four bastards lyin' over there."

"You killed them?" one of the young men asked. Both of them were crying now, too.

The Kid nodded. "They didn't give us much choice. They must have been members of Latch's gang."

The man lying on the ground finally stopped sobbing enough to look up and say, "Latch? Warren Latch?"

"You know him, mister?" Culhane asked quickly.

"No, I . . . I've just heard of him. The newspapers say he's a madman."

"I reckon they're right," Culhane said grimly. He started forward. "Lemme give you a hand. We'll get in out of this sun."

"My wife and my girls can't," the man said, his voice bitter and hurt. "They have to lie out here in it."

"I know it ain't much comfort, but they're past hurtin' now."

The man struggled to his feet and pawed at his eyes with the back of a work-roughened hand. He was an older version of the two young men, with graying fair hair and a mustache.

"I've forgotten . . . my hospitality. Come on in

my house. I'll see if we can . . . rustle up something to eat."

"That ain't necessary," Culhane assured him. "But we'll go in and talk about this."

Culhane put a hand on the man's arm. He didn't pull away. The Ranger led him toward the house.

One of the two young men asked The Kid, "What happened to old Tip? Looks like he was shot pretty recent-like."

The Kid answered the question honestly. "One of our men put him down. We didn't know if anybody was coming back, and he didn't want to leave the dog here to starve. It was his idea. Ranger Culhane didn't order it. But the hombre was just trying to . . . do a kindness."

He didn't mention Reilly's other comment about how the dog had nothing left to love.

Reilly had been wrong about that.

The young man knelt beside the dog and stroked a hand over the shaggy coat. His voice was choked as he said, "So long, Tip. I know you did everything you could to protect Ma and the girls."

"Come on, Thad," the other young man said. "We ought to go with Pa and make sure he's all right."

Thad nodded, forcing himself back to his feet.

They started toward the ranch house with The Kid. Thad said, "My name's Thad Gustaffson. This is my brother Bill. Our pa's Abel."

"Morgan," The Kid introduced himself.

As they passed the open barn door, he called to the men inside. "The trouble's over. See to your horses. We'll be riding soon."

Ed Marchman stepped into view, cradling his rifle. "Mighty quick to start giving orders, aren't you, Morgan?" the man asked in an unpleasant tone.

"It's not an order, Marchman," The Kid said. "Just common sense."

Nick Burton stepped out of the barn and nodded. "We'll do what you say, Mr. Morgan." He turned and called to his grandfather's hands. "M-B Connected, let's go!"

It wasn't the strongest tone of command The Kid had ever heard . . . but it was a start, he thought with a faint smile.

"My wife's name was Molly," Abel Gustaffson said. "The twins were Helen and Paula." He took a gulp from the glass of whiskey in front of him as he sat at a rough-hewn table in one side of the double cabin. He had taken the bottle from a cabinet. "They were seventeen."

"I'm sure sorry," Culhane said. "For what it's worth, which I know ain't a whole hell of a lot, I don't reckon any of 'em suffered much."

"They weren't . . . mistreated?"

"No, sir, not a bit."

That was a bald-faced lie, The Kid thought . . .

but he would have answered Gustaffson the same way Culhane had. It wouldn't change a damned thing for the man to know the sort of hell his daughters had gone through before they died.

And at least it was true about Molly Gustaffson. The Kid had found a pitchfork in the barn with dried blood on the tines and assumed she had been killed with it. He figured she had died fairly quickly.

"The boys and I drove some cattle down to the shipping pens on the railroad, about thirty miles south of here," Gustaffson went on, obviously feeling the need to explain why the three women had been alone. "I knew we'd only be gone for a few days, and we've never had any trouble before. It's not like we have to worry about Comanches or anything like that, the way folks used to."

"No, sir, that's right," Culhane said from the other side of the table. "There was no way you could have known what was gonna happen. No way on God's green earth."

"Molly is . . . was . . ." Gustaffson had to stop and draw a breath before he could go on. "She was cool-headed, and a good shot. She'd killed wolves with that old Henry before. I thought . . . they would be all right."

"We all did, Pa," Bill Gustaffson said.

The rancher looked across the table at Culhane. "Did you say proper words over them?"

"I tried, sir. I did my level best. We all did. They was laid to rest with respect."

"Thank you for that," Gustaffson murmured. He looked over at The Kid, who had turned around one of the chairs and straddled it. "And thank you for killing the miserable scum that did this."

"They got what was coming to them," The Kid said. "Probably more mercy than they deserved, because they died fast."

Gustaffson nodded. "But the rest of that bunch of devils . . . they got away."

"Not for good," Culhane promised. "We're fixin' to get on their trail again, Mr. Gustaffson. We'll see to it they're brought to justice."

"You won't go alone," Gustaffson declared. "We're coming with you."

"That's right," Thad said, and Bill nodded.

"Now hold on." Culhane said. "You can't—"

"Why not?" Gustaffson cut in. His face was still streaked with dried tears, but his terrible sorrow had settled down into a deep and abiding rage.

The Kid recognized that. He had experienced the same thing more than once in his life.

"Are you gonna say we can't go with you, Ranger?" Gustaffson asked. "Why in blazes shouldn't we?"

"I know you want vengeance, Mr. Gustaffson, but you should leave that to us," Culhane insisted.

"Didn't you say half the men in your posse came along because Latch and his men burned down their homes and businesses and killed their loved ones? My house is still standing, but the pain these boys and I feel is just as deep as anybody else's in that posse!"

"We're not out for vengeance any more than they are, Ranger," Thad added.

Culhane couldn't argue with that. After a moment, he nodded. "All right. You're welcome to come along, and I'll be honest with you, I'll be glad to have three more guns. But what about your ranch?"

"You're headed east, right?"

"Yeah."

"We'll pass a neighbor's spread a few miles from here. I can get him to look after the place while we're gone."

Bill Gustaffson suddenly looked alarmed. "Doris!" he exclaimed.

"That's the gal my brother's been courtin' on that other spread," Thad explained. "He's worried Latch and his men might have stopped there, too."

Culhane put his hands on the table and shoved himself to his feet. "We'd best get a move on then, so we can find out. You fellas best pack some supplies, if you got 'em. Do you have any fresh horses?"

Gustaffson nodded. "We'll be ready to ride in a few minutes, Ranger."

Thad said, "I'm burying Tip before I go any-where."

"Put him next . . . next to your ma, son," Gustaffson choked out. "He was always her dog more than anybody else's."

"I'll help you, Thad," The Kid offered.

Thad started to refuse with a stubborn shake of his head. Then he said, "I'm obliged, Morgan. Let's go."

As they walked out of the cabin and started toward the gravesite, Thad went on, "Which one of the posse shot him?"

"You don't need to know that," The Kid replied. "It wouldn't do any good."

Thad glared at him. "Was it you?"

"No. I don't think I would have done that."

After a second, Thad shrugged. "No, I don't reckon you would have."

Nick came out of the barn to join them. "Can I give you a hand, Mr. Morgan?"

"I think that would be fine, Nick." The Kid performed the introductions. "Nick Burton, Thad Gustaffson."

"I'm sure sorry about . . . about everything, Thad," Nick said.

"Thanks. We're gonna bury our dog." Thad drew in a deep, ragged breath. "You have a dog, Nick?"

"No. I did for a while when I was a little kid, but he got sick and died."

"Sorry," Thad muttered.

The Kid hung back a little to let the two

youngsters talk. Tragedy sometimes brought people together and made them friends. It had happened in his case, and those friendships had helped him get through some mighty rough times. Maybe it would be like that with Nick and Thad.

Less than half an hour later the posse, stronger by three, rode out and took up the trail of the outlaws.

CHAPTER 13

"How long do you think it'll take Cooper and the others to catch up to us?" Duval asked as he and Latch rode at the head of the big group of riders.

"They had better catch up by the end of the day," Latch snapped. "All they had to do was finish off those girls, kill all the livestock they could find, and burn everything to the ground. That shouldn't have taken them more than an hour or two."

If that was all they had done, Duval mused.

Cooper was a pretty good man, but Rattigan was one of the four Latch had assigned to handle the mopping up. Like the creature that formed part of his name, Rattigan was a particularly loathsome vermin, even for that bunch of cutthroats. He was sly, too, and had a way of wheedling other men into going along with what he wanted.

The other two outlaws who'd been left behind

at the ranch, Fellows and Clark, were easily led. Duval could easily see Rattigan persuading them they ought to have another go at the twins before they killed the girls, and with the three of them united, Cooper would have had to go along with them.

But maybe he was worrying for nothing, Duval told himself. Maybe the four men would do exactly what they were supposed to do and nothing more, and by nightfall they would have come galloping up to rejoin the rest of the gang. It didn't make any sense to go borrowing trouble.

By late afternoon, though, when Latch and Duval began looking for a good place to camp, there had been no sign of Cooper and the others. Duval saw familiar sparks of anger in Latch's eyes, a bad sign.

The plains through which they had ridden for the past several days were starting to peter out into a stretch of rugged, wooded hills and canyons. Several more days of riding through the rougher terrain lay between them and San Antonio, which was situated where the landscape became flatter again and started to turn into the coastal plain running all the way to the Gulf of Mexico.

Latch found a hollow he liked the looks of and announced, "We'll camp here for the night."

The rest of the men immediately dismounted and set to work tending to the horses, gathering wood for a fire, and setting up camp.

Latch stalked to the top of the ridge that formed one side of the hollow and stopped, peering back to the west, the direction from which they had come.

Seeing that, Duval went up to join him. "Looking for Cooper and the others?"

"They should have caught up to us by now," Latch snapped. "They've disobeyed my orders."

He wasn't worried about the possibility that something had happened to the four men, Duval realized. The thing that bothered Latch was the chance somebody hadn't done exactly what he'd told them to do.

"Maybe they decided they've had enough of riding with us and went off on their own," Duval suggested.

"Without their share of the loot?" Latch shook his head. "I don't think so. One thing all my men have in common is greed."

He was probably right about that, Duval had to admit.

"No, it's more likely they lingered there to enjoy themselves some more with those girls," Latch went on. "I told them not to waste any more time. But that man Rattigan is scum. Clever scum, but still scum."

Latch was thinking along the same lines Duval had, earlier in the day.

But so much time had passed, he didn't think that was a satisfactory explanation anymore.

"Even if they had, it wouldn't have taken them all day, boss. They still should have caught up to us by now."

Latch jerked his head in a curt nod. "Yes. Something has happened to them."

"Maybe that posse from Fire Hill is still after us. Maybe they rode up to that ranch while Cooper and the others were still there and caught them."

Latch frowned. "Those men should have turned back by now. We've never had a posse chase us for this long."

"We never burned down a whole town before, either," Duval pointed out.

Latch stroked his beard and smiled in obvious pleasure at the memory of all those buildings going up in flames as the crackling roar was accompanied by shrill screams. "That's true, Slim," he said softly. "We never did."

He straightened and took a deep breath. "We need to find out for certain. Can you follow our back trail at night?"

"I reckon I can," Duval said.

"Take three men with you and scout behind us," Latch ordered. "I want to know if that posse is back there, and if they are, how close they are. Can you do that, Slim?"

"Of course I can," Duval answered without hesitation. He didn't particularly relish the job, but if that's what Latch wanted him to do, he would try his best. To do otherwise would be too dangerous, and Slim Duval was a cautious man.

"Good. I assumed they would turn back after we hit them before. Men like that get worked up and join a posse, but as soon as they realize it could get them killed, their courage evaporates. If this bunch is being particularly stubborn, we may have to take steps."

"Steps?" Duval repeated.

"That's right. We may have to stop long enough to wipe them out."

By nightfall, Abel Gustaffson and his sons had settled into an attitude of stoic, stolid grief. It matched what the other members of the posse from Fire Hill had felt a few days earlier when their homes had been destroyed and their loved ones killed.

That pain had dulled slightly for them with the passage of time, but it was still fresh for the father and his two sons.

That was the thing about pain, The Kid mused as the men went about the work of setting up camp. It never went away completely. For days at a time, you might not think about everything you'd lost in life, but then something unexpected would remind you and you'd feel that all-too-familiar twinge deep inside, like somebody had just poked you in the vitals with a knife.

Maybe by the time thirty or forty or fifty years had passed, those feelings finally went away. The

Kid hadn't lived that long yet and didn't really expect to, the way he kept getting mixed up in things where people shot at him.

But somehow he doubted that grief ever really died.

Nick was hanging around with Thad Gustaffson, and his brother Bill had joined them. The Kid figured it was probably good for all of them.

Some of Bill's worries had been eased when the posse stopped at the neighboring ranch and found that Latch's gang hadn't been there. Doris Horton, the pretty brunette eighteen-year-old Bill had been courting, was fine.

She and her mother and her sisters had all cried when they heard what had happened at the Gustaffson ranch. Doris's father J. W. Horton had shaken Abel Gustaffson's hand, slapped him encouragingly on the back, and solemnly promised to look after Abel's place for as long as necessary.

"If we're not back in a couple weeks, consider it yours, J.W.," Gustaffson had told him. "You've been a mighty good friend and neighbor to us, and I don't know anybody else I'd rather see take over the place."

"Now, don't be talkin' like that," Horton had told him. "You'll be runnin' your own ranch again before you know it. You and the boys are gonna come back and be just fine."

Gustaffson hadn't had anything to say to that.

They might come back, The Kid mused, but he doubted if they would ever really be fine again.

After that side trip to the Horton ranch, the posse had picked up the trail of the outlaws again and put quite a few more miles behind them.

As The Kid sat beside Culhane at the campfire that evening, the Ranger said, "Another day, maybe less, and we'll start gettin' into the hill country. Ever been there, Morgan?"

The Kid shook his head. "Like I told you, I've been to San Antonio, but I don't know that much about the rest of Texas."

"It's a land of . . . what do you call it? . . . infinite variety," Culhane said with the note of pride in his voice common to people who had been borned and raised in the Lone Star State. "Just about any kind of country you're lookin' for, you can find it here. Just about every kind of people, too. Most of 'em are good, hard-workin' folks. For them that ain't . . . well, that's why we got the Rangers."

"Where did Latch come from?"

"Georgia. His folks brought him and the rest of the family here after the war, when Latch was just a little shaver. They'd lost pert near everything when ol' William Tecumseh Sherman came marchin' through, and then the Yankee carpetbaggers come in and took the little bit that was left. Made Latch's pa pretty bitter, I expect. He settled the family over in East Texas, close to

Nacogdoches. I don't care for that piney country. Too woody and snaky for my tastes.

"Anyway, that's about all I know. I got a hunch Latch was a mite off in the head all along. A fella don't go that loco overnight. When we sent Rangers over to Nacogdoches to find out if any of his family that's still there had seen him lately, they heard stories about some of the things he done as a kid growin' up."

Culhane shook his head. "The neighbors learned mighty quick to keep their own kids and their pets away from that Latch boy."

"You wouldn't think somebody like that would be able to put together such a big gang and manage to avoid being caught for so long," The Kid commented.

"Just because a fella's plumb crazy don't mean he ain't plenty smart, too."

The Kid knew that was true. In his past, he had been plagued by a vengeance-seeking woman who had been cruelly insane, but also cunning enough to wreak havoc in his life on several occasions, in several different ways.

It was a good thing Pamela Tarleton had never met Warren Latch, he mused. If those two had ever gotten together, the results might have been too horrifying to contemplate.

But Pamela was dead, and with any luck Warren Latch soon would be, too, or at least safely locked up behind bars.

The men began to turn in for the night, except for the ones who would be standing guard. The Kid had one of the middle shifts, so he rolled into his blankets and went to sleep.

Woody Anderson, the burly blacksmith from Fire Hill with the wounded arm, woke him when it was his turn to be on watch.

"Everything quiet, Woody?" The Kid asked.

Anderson nodded. "Yeah, nothin' stirrin' out there tonight." The man's voice was a rumble, even when he was trying to be quiet.

The Kid clapped a hand on the shoulder of Anderson's good arm. "Fine. Go get some sleep."

He picked up his Winchester and walked out beyond the small ring of light cast by the fire, which had burned down to embers, giving off only a feeble glow.

Plenty of stars and a sickle-shaped moon revealed the landscape around him. A couple hundred yards from the camp, The Kid found a small knoll where he could sit down.

Culhane had said the posse would reach the end of the plains the next day, but for tonight, they were still surrounded by flat prairie dotted with brush and an occasional stand of scrubby trees. The hardy grass was starting to turn brown from the summer heat and lack of rain.

All The Kid's senses were alert as he sat there watching, listening, and even smelling the night. His instincts were on keen edge. He had no real reason to think the posse might be attacked, but the possibility always existed that Latch might double back and try to ambush them.

Other, unknown dangers could be lurking out there in the night, too. It never hurt to be careful.

Because even when you were, things could happen.

Terrible things.

Because he was so on edge and just waiting for trouble, it wasn't surprising that a little while later The Kid heard a noise, the sort of faint sound most men wouldn't hear and wouldn't think anything of if they did.

It was only a tiny *clink,* but he knew it was the sound of a horseshoe hitting a rock.

Somebody was out there.

CHAPTER 14

Briefly, The Kid considered waking Culhane, but he didn't want to disturb the Ranger's sleep for something that might turn out to be nothing.

The rider he'd heard might be a lone cowboy just drifting past in the night, on his way back to an isolated ranch from a night in town . . . although The Kid didn't know what settlements, if any, were around there.

Deciding it would be better to get some more information before raising an alarm, he slid down from the knoll and moved silently into a small stand of trees. The thick shadows under the branches completely concealed him as he waited tensely to see if anyone was coming closer to the camp.

A few minutes later, not just one rider but several men on horseback moved into The Kid's view. The light was not good. It was hard for him to tell how many shadowy figures there were. Three or four, he thought.

They reined in not far from him, and he heard one of them say in a half whisper, "I tell you, I saw the glow from a campfire up ahead a little ways, Slim."

"I believe you," the man called Slim said. "It's got to be that damned posse, just like the boss thought. But we'd better make sure. I suppose it might be a caravan of freight wagons or something like that."

In the stygian darkness under the trees, The Kid stiffened at the words he had just overheard. He had no doubt the men were members of Latch's gang. The boss outlaw must have sent them back to scout for the posse and find out how far behind the pursuit was.

It would be easy enough to bring the Winchester to his shoulder and open fire on them, The Kid thought. Shooting was tricky in bad light, even at short range, but there was a good chance he could bring down all of them.

But if he waited and continued to spy on them, they might say something else that would come in handy to know.

He was confident they weren't going to ambush the camp. Since there were only four of them— The Kid was certain of that number now that he could see them better—starting a fight with a group the size of the posse would be foolhardy.

"If it is the posse, you think they got Cooper and the others prisoner?" one of the other men asked.

"Not likely," Slim replied. "The fellas would've put up a fight. Anyway, after seeing what happened to those women, the posse wouldn't have been in any mood to take prisoners. They'd have strung those poor bastards up to the nearest tree."

Slim was right about that, The Kid thought, although it was possible Culhane would have tried to insist the men be held for trial.

But even a Texas Ranger's will might not prevail in a situation like that.

"No, if those boys were still at the ranch when the posse got there, they're dead now," Slim continued. "I just hope they took some of the posse with 'em."

Too bad, Slim, The Kid thought. That hadn't happened . . . and the four outlaws were lying in a shallow grave, which was more than they deserved. Leaving them for the buzzards and the coyotes would have been more fitting.

"What do we do now?" one of the men asked.

"I want to get a little closer," Slim said. "When I tell Warren what we found, I want to know as much as I possibly can about that posse."

More than ever, The Kid wanted to start blasting away at them. They were partially responsible for what had happened to Molly, Paula, and Helen Gustaffson, not to mention all the death and devastation back in Fire Hill.

Though The Kid hadn't witnessed that destruction firsthand, the memory of how he had found the three women earlier in the day was still very fresh in his mind. If anybody ever deserved some hot lead justice, it was those four skunks.

However, they might be more valuable in the long run if they could be taken prisoner and made to reveal what they knew about Latch's plans.

That was uppermost in The Kid's mind as he moved soundlessly to the edge of the trees and watched the men dismount. One man took the reins of all four horses while the other three outlaws crept closer to the camp on foot.

Watching his companions sneak closer to the camp, the man holding the horse never saw The Kid creeping up soundlessly behind him. As he came within arm's length, The Kid raised the Winchester to ram the rifle's butt against the back of the man's head.

But before he could strike, someone shouted, "Hey, who are you fel—"

Gunshots interrupted the startled cry, but The

Kid had heard enough to recognize the voice. It belonged to Nick Burton. The Kid didn't know if Nick was standing guard, or if he'd just gotten up to relieve himself or something like that.

Either way, Nick was in the middle of plenty of trouble.

The Kid finished the blow he had started to launch. The butt of his Winchester crashed against the back of the outlaw's head. The man let go of the horses' reins and dropped like a rock.

Suddenly freed, and startled by the shout and the gunshots, the horses bolted. Leaping back quickly, The Kid managed to avoid being trampled.

As soon as the animals were out of his way, he ran toward the sounds of battle. Muzzle flashes split the darkness, but there was no way to tell who was firing until he got closer.

With no warning, a rapidly moving shape charged out of the night and collided with The Kid. They caromed off each other, the impact causing The Kid to drop his rifle as he fell to the ground.

The other man lost his footing, too. As he rolled over and came up, a stream of Spanish obscenities poured from his mouth. The Kid had met everybody in the posse and none of them were Mexican, so the Spanish curses pegged the man as one of the outlaws.

The man drew his arm back and flashed it forward, further proving his hostile intent. Only

The Kid's almost superhuman reflexes saved him as he jerked out of the path of the knife whipping past him.

The Kid palmed out his Colt and brought it up, hesitating for a second. If his opponent was armed only with the knife, he ought to be able to take him prisoner.

The man clawed at his hip, eliminating that possibility. Starlight flickered on the barrel of a gun as the weapon cleared leather.

The Kid didn't wait any longer. He fired, flame licking from the barrel of the revolver in his hand.

The bullet smashed into the outlaw's chest and drove him backward. His finger clenched on the trigger of his gun in a dying spasm, but the bullet went harmlessly into the ground at his feet. He landed on his back in the loose sprawl of death.

"There they go! Get 'em!"

That was Culhane's voice. The Kid heard pounding footsteps and realized the other two outlaws were fleeing straight toward him as fast as they could.

The posse members had taken a few moments to get their wits about them after they'd been jolted out of sleep, but now they were awake and ready to fight. A barrage of shots directed at the remaining two outlaws lit up the night.

Unfortunately, The Kid was in the path of the posse's bullets, as well. He threw himself forward and hit the dirt, making himself as small a target as possible as lead shredded the air above his head.

One of the outlaws howled in pain and threw his arms out to the sides as he stumbled, driven ahead by the slugs slamming into his back. When he lost his balance he pitched forward and landed face-down on the ground, practically beside The Kid.

The other man remained unhit, protected from the storm of bullets by a providence he didn't deserve. The Kid snapped a shot at him with the Colt, but the man kept moving fast as before.

A couple seconds later The Kid heard hoofbeats. Coming across one of the horses left behind, the outlaw had grabbed it and leaped into the saddle. Over the shots fired by the posse men The Kid heard the drumming of the horses's hooves on the prairie. The animal wasn't slowing down.

"Hold your fire! Hold your fire! It's Morgan!"

He had to yell a couple more times before Culhane heard him and bellowed, "Hold your fire, blast it! We got one of our men out there!"

The shooting trailed off and then stopped completely. The Kid was still cautious as he poked his head up and called, "It's me, Morgan! I'm coming in!"

He got to his feet, looked around for a minute, and found his rifle lying where he had dropped it. As he walked up to the campsite, someone stirred the fire back to life and added some wood to it. Flames leaped up, casting a circle of light.

Culhane didn't have his hat or his boots on, but his gun was in his hand. Stepping up to The Kid, he asked, "What happened out there?"

"Latch sent four men back to spy on us," The Kid explained. "I happened to hear them coming and was able to get behind them. I was going to try to capture them, but then Nick yelled and the shooting started." The Kid looked around at the gathered posse members. "I don't see Nick. Is he all right?"

A slight figure pushed between two of the other men and stepped forward.

"Yeah, I'm all right, Mr. Morgan," Nick Burton said. "Those outlaws shot at me when I saw them, but I was lucky. They didn't hit me."

"What were you doin' up, son?" Culhane asked. "It wasn't your turn to stand guard."

"I, uh, couldn't sleep," Nick said uncomfortably. "I had to go off in the bushes and, uh, tend to some business."

"Did you tell anybody before you went to tend to that *business?*" Culhane asked.

"Well . . . no."

"Then you're lucky one of our own guards didn't ventilate you, let alone them owlhoots!" Culhane said. "Don't go skulkin' around in the dark, boy. It's a good way to get killed."

Nick swallowed hard and nodded. "Yes, sir,

130

Ranger Culhane. I'll remember that from now on."

"See that you do," Culhane said with a disgusted snort. He turned back to The Kid. "Did they all get away?"

"Only one of them," The Kid said. "And I knocked one of them out, so maybe we can get him to tell us exactly where Latch is heading."

"Give the prisoner . . . to me," Vint Reilly rasped. "I'll make him talk."

"Take it easy, Reilly," Culhane said. "Let me put my boots on, Morgan, and we'll fetch in this fella."

A couple minutes later, Culhane and The Kid started toward the man who had been holding the horses. Thad Gustaffson and Jack Hogan went along, carrying burning branches plucked from the fire. It didn't take them long to find the man who was lying facedown in the dirt.

Culhane knelt and rolled him over. The man's eyes stared up sightlessly into the torchlight.

"Damn it," The Kid burst out. "I didn't think I hit him that hard."

Culhane lifted the outlaw's head and felt the back of it. "Yep, his skull's stove in, all right. You might not've done it, though, Morgan. The way those horses were stampedin' around out here, one of them could've stepped on him."

That was true, The Kid supposed. Actually it was a more likely explanation. It was a stroke of bad luck, though. He'd been counting on getting some information from the prisoner.

Now they just had three more dead outlaws to bury, instead of two.

Unless Culhane decided to leave them for the carrion eaters this time.

CHAPTER 15

Duval was still a little shaken by the time he got back to the outlaw camp, long after midnight.

On several occasions in his violent past, he had come close enough to dying to hear the whine of a bullet close to his head, but never in his life had he experienced the sheer terror of being caught in a volley like the one that had shot Al Haskins to pieces.

Even though several hours had passed since then, Duval still found it hard to believe he wasn't dead, too. Slugs had been humming around him like he had blundered into a swarm of bees. Yet not one of them had touched him.

He had a guardian angel looking out for him, he supposed. That was the only explanation.

Although considering the things he had done in his life, a guardian devil was more likely . . .

He reined to a halt on top of the ridge overlooking the hollow and called softly, "Hello, the camp!"

"Who's that?" one of the guards challenged him.

Duval recognized Ortiz's voice. "It's me. Duval."

"Slim?" Holding a rifle, Ortiz stepped out from behind the tree where he had been standing. "Is that you? Where are the three hombres who went with you?"

"Dead, is my best guess," Duval said grimly. "I have to talk to the boss."

Ortiz shook his head. "I don't envy you that job, amigo."

Duval snorted and rode on down the slope into the camp. His arrival disturbed some of the sleeping men, who roused up enough to curse bitterly.

Duval asked, "Where's the boss?"

"I'm here," Latch said as he strode forward. He knelt beside the embers of the fire and stirred them up so the red glow they gave off lit his face.

The man had never looked more like Satan himself, Duval thought.

Latch straightened to his feet and snapped, "What did you find out? Where are the other men?"

"The posse's back there, all right," Duval reported. "About five miles behind us. I'm sorry, Warren. They killed Haskins, Jonah, and Sanchez."

Latch stiffened. His eyes widened with anger as he stepped toward Duval. "You weren't supposed to engage them, just find out where they were."

"I know that. It wasn't my idea to trade shots with them. One of the bastards was out wandering around in the brush where we didn't expect any-body to be. He grabbed for a gun, and Sanchez panicked and started shooting at him. That got the whole camp mixed up in it." Duval paused. "I'm damned lucky to be alive, Warren. The bullets were as thick as flies around me. But I knew I had to make it back here to report to you."

"So that excuses fleeing and leaving those other men behind to die?"

Duval's pride wouldn't allow him to meekly accept the implication of cowardice in Latch's sharply worded question. His own voice was sharp as he replied, "They were already down, shot to pieces, before I got out of there. I didn't see how it would do any good for me to die there, too."

What he said wasn't strictly, completely true. He had seen Al Haskins cut down and knew the man had to be dead. Nobody carried around that much lead and lived. And since the horses were loose, he had assumed that young Jonah was done for, as well.

But he hadn't seen Sanchez's body. That was worrisome. If Sanchez was alive, and that posse had him, they might force him to talk.

Duval wasn't going to say anything about that and give Latch even more of a reason to be mad at him.

Anyway, there wasn't really that much Sanchez could reveal about their plans. He knew they were headed for San Antonio, but hell, anybody who knew east from west could tell that much just by following the gang's trail.

Since they all split up before they reached the city, nobody knew where more than one or two of the others could be found. That was the beauty of operating the way they did.

Latch glared at Duval for a few seconds more, then abruptly stepped forward and rested a hand on the Cajun's shoulder. Duval had to force himself not to flinch.

"You're right, Slim," Latch said as the anger disappeared from his lean face and no longer burned in his deep-set eyes. "It wouldn't have done any good for you to die, too. And it shows your loyalty that you were determined to live so you could warn us about the posse."

Latch looked around at the members of the gang who had gathered to hear what Duval had to say. "Isn't that right, men?"

He got mutters of agreement, and one of the men even pitched in with a half-hearted, "Good job, Slim."

"You must be tired," Latch went on. "You need to get some rest now."

"What are we going to do about that posse?" Duval asked.

"You said they're five miles behind us?"

"About that, yeah."

"We don't have to worry about them catching up to us tonight," Latch declared. "It appears we're going to have to try again to discourage them from following us, though. I'll think about it and decide what form that discouragement should take."

Satisfied that he was still alive and Latch didn't seem to be too upset with him, Duval figured it was better to quit while he was ahead. "That sounds good to me, boss. I'll turn in, like you suggested."

"Sleep well, Slim." Latch smiled coldly. "After all, you could be sleeping permanently right now."

The next morning, Culhane insisted they put the three dead outlaws in a shallow grave, just as The Kid expected he would.

"It may not keep the coyotes from diggin' 'em up," Culhane said, "but at least we made the effort, and that's one thing that separates us from animals like them."

"When you say animals, do you mean the coyotes . . . or the outlaws?" The Kid asked.

The Ranger grunted. "Take your pick. Personally, I reckon the coyotes are a mite more honorable than Latch's varmints. They don't have the excuse of bein' what passes for human."

When the burial was finished, Abel Gustaffson took off his hat and stepped up to the mound of dirt marking the final resting place of the three outlaws. Everybody else stepped back, giving the grief-stricken man room to do whatever it was he intended to do.

Gustaffson stood there for a long moment, holding his hat in one hand. Then he spat on the grave.

His sons started toward him, but Vint Reilly got there first. The badly burned man laid a bandaged hand on Gustaffson's shoulder and spoke to him in gravelly tones too low for any of the other men to understand.

Gustaffson seemed to agree with whatever Reilly was saying. After a moment he nodded, and both men turned away from the grave.

"Let's go," Reilly said in his tortured voice. "We've got . . . outlaws to catch."

As the members of the posse mounted up and moved out, Culhane took the lead as usual and waved a hand for The Kid to join him. "Those fellas showin' up the way they did means Latch is worried about us followin' him. Since one of 'em got away, chances are he knows by now how far behind him we are."

"You're not telling me anything I haven't already thought about, Ranger," The Kid said. "The odds of us riding into an ambush just went up, didn't they?"

Culhane nodded. "We got to be more careful than ever, especially since so many of the fellas with us are greenhorns when it comes to huntin' owlhoots. I been keepin' an eye on you, Morgan.

I can tell by the way you carry yourself, you've packed a badge before, haven't you?"

The Kid laughed. Just the opposite was true, in fact. He had been in prison—unjustly, sure, but still, he'd been there—and he had been a wanted fugitive with a bounty on his head.

"Well, maybe you ain't ever been an official lawman, but I know this ain't the first manhunt you've been part of. You're a top-notch fightin' man, and you're the second-in-command of this posse now."

"I didn't ask for that job," The Kid said sharply.

"I know you didn't, but I'm givin' it to you anyway. If anything happens to me, you're in charge, and I'm countin' on you gettin' the job done."

The Kid glanced over his shoulder at the riders strung out behind them. In a low voice, he said, "You're putting me in charge of some grieving townies, a bunch of cowpokes, a wet-behind-the-ears kid, and a man who's burned so bad he ought to be in a hospital, not to mention he's maybe more than a little bit loco. With that group we're going to track down and kill or capture a small army of cold-blooded killers and gunmen. Is that about the size of it?"

Culhane grinned. "No need to thank me."

The Kid grunted and shook his head.

The Ranger grew serious. "If something happens

to me and you don't take over, Morgan . . . who will?"

"Reilly, maybe. He seems to be about as driven as anybody I've ever seen. He'd have to be in order to keep going, the shape he's in. And maybe Gustaffson would be his segundo."

"Wouldn't work," Culhane snapped. "Yeah, those two are bound and determined to catch Latch, but they got too much hate burnin' 'em up inside. They can't think straight without somebody else tellin' 'em what to do. Leave it up to them and they'd pull some damn fool stunt like chargin' into a trap and gettin' themselves and everybody else killed." The Ranger paused. "I mean it, Morgan. I need to know you'll step in if you have to."

The Kid could have kicked himself for doing it, but he nodded. "All right, Culhane. I'll take over if I have to."

"Your word on it?"

"My word on it," The Kid said.

"All right. I'm much obliged to you, Morgan, I'll tell you that. I'll let the others know later, when we stop, that you're in charge if anything happens to me."

"There's no guarantee they'll all go along with the idea," The Kid pointed out.

"They will if they know what's good for 'em."

That was just it, The Kid thought. Some of the posse were so blinded by hate and grief they didn't know what was good for them. It was a situation he knew well. He'd found himself in it more than once.

As the trail they were following neared the edge of the hill country, which was marked by a green line of thicker vegetation on the horizon, The Kid spotted smoke rising to the north. It wasn't the billowing black clouds of something on fire, but rather several thin white columns of chimney smoke.

He pointed them out to Culhane. "Looks like a little settlement over there."

The Ranger nodded and waved a hand toward the tracks, which continued angling to the southeast.

"Yeah, but Latch and his bunch went around it. I reckon those folks who live over there don't know how lucky they are. It's like havin' a tornado skip past you on a stormy night without you ever seein' it."

Except that a raid by Warren Latch and his gang was an unnatural disaster, not a natural one, The Kid thought, but he understood what Culhane meant and agreed with it.

He and the Ranger weren't the only ones who had spotted the settlement. Buildings were visible in the distance, and Ed Marchman rode up and pointed at them. "We need supplies, Culhane. You know we couldn't salvage much from what was left of Fire Hill, and we've been on short rations pretty much the whole way."

"That's true," Culhane admitted, "but that settlement's out of our way."

"My God, it's just right over there! Probably not more than half a mile. It wouldn't take us long to see if we can pick up some provisions. Good Lord, you'd think if we can take the time to bury some murderous outlaws, we can take the time to get some food."

Culhane glanced at The Kid, who shrugged. He wasn't in charge yet, and the decision was still the Ranger's to make.

"I reckon you're right, Marchman," Culhane admitted. "We'll ride over there and see if there's a general store." His voice hardened. "But if there's a saloon in that town, it's off-limits, understand? We ain't gonna take the time for anybody to guzzle down any tonsil varnish."

"That's fine with me," Marchman said. "I just want some supplies."

Culhane signaled for the men to rein in. He pointed out the settlement, which all of them had already noticed anyway. "We'll stop for a few minutes and pick up some supplies. But that's all. When I say we hit the trail, we hit the trail. Got it?"

Several of the men nodded. Marchman said, "We understand, Ranger."

Culhane waved them into motion again. The posse rode toward the settlement at a trot.

After being on the trail for several days, the men were anxious for the sight of a town again.

It would probably just remind them of everything they had lost, The Kid mused. As they approached the settlement, he saw that it didn't amount to much. There were two lines of buildings, a mixture of houses and businesses, facing each other for a distance of a couple hundred yards. A public well stood at one end of the street, a small church at the other. That was it.

But there was a store—BRENNAMAN'S TRADING POST AND EMPORIUM, according to the sign on the front of the building—and that was all that mattered.

The Kid noticed a blacksmith shop as well and wondered if any of the horses had shoes that needed tending to. That would take more time, but it might mean less trouble later.

Another building bore the sign HAMPTON'S SALOON—LIQUOR AND CIGARS. Culhane wanted the men to avoid the saloon, but that might be difficult to manage. Some of the cowboys from the M-B Connected were already looking mighty thirsty.

The Ranger headed for the store and said over his shoulder, "All right, everybody follow me now. We ain't got much time—"

He stopped short as the trading post's front door opened and a woman hurried out onto the building's high porch. The sun flashed on red hair under her hat. Two men emerged from the building right behind her, moving fast. One of them reached out and grabbed her arm.

"Hold on there, lady!" he said in a loud, raucous voice. "Hell, Rudy and me are just tryin' to be friendly."

The woman tried to pull away. "Let go of me!"

The two men laughed, and the second one reached for her as well.

They weren't laughing a second later when the metallic sound of The Kid's revolver being cocked cut through the air. They looked around in surprise as he leveled the Colt at them and said coldly, "You heard the lady. Let her go."

CHAPTER 16

He was being showy, and he knew it. The Colt was a double-action model. He didn't have to cock it in order to fire it. All he had to do was pull the trigger.

But at the same time, it was an effective tactic. The sound of a gun being cocked was enough to freeze the blood of many men.

It was in this case. As the two men stared at The Kid, their hands fell away from the woman.

She stepped away from them, straightened her clothes, and sniffed disdainfully. Her auburn hair was cut short under the bottle-green hat she wore. A traveling dress of the same shade hugged the supple curves of her body. She wasn't classically beautiful, but had an undeniable attractiveness about her that instantly drew a man's eye and held it.

Beside The Kid, Culhane said, "Morgan, what are you doin'? This is none of our business."

"I can't stand by and do nothing while a woman's being mistreated, Ranger. Can you?"

"Well, now that you mention it . . . no. But we don't need to be gettin' in any gunfights with these folks, either."

"There's not going to be any gunfight." The Kid's lips curved in an icy smile as he looked at the two men on the store's porch. "Is there?"

The men were typical small-town roughnecks, the sort who worked at odd jobs part of the time and stayed drunk the rest. But they wore guns, and they could be dangerous.

One of them said belligerently, "You got no call to mix in this, mister. We weren't gonna hurt the lady. We just thought she might be willin' to give us a kiss. We don't see many like her here in Stubbtown."

"I'll give you something." The redhead stepped closer to the men and brought her hand up in a pair of stinging slaps that cracked across the men's faces. "That's what I'll give you!"

They fell back a step, probably more shocked by the blows than they were hurt. The woman glared at them for a second before turning away as if they were beneath contempt.

She nodded to The Kid. "Thank you, sir. It's not often one encounters such gallantry out here on this rude frontier."

"You're welcome, ma'am." He lowered the hammer on his gun and pouched the iron. Moving the buckskin closer to the porch, he went on, "Can I see you safely to your destination?"

Culhane said, "Morgan, blast it—"

"Why, thank you," the redhead told The Kid with a smile. "That would be very nice."

That wasn't how it worked out, though. With a roar of anger, one of the humiliated roughnecks let his wounded pride get the best of him now that The Kid's gun was holstered. The man got a running start by taking a couple steps and launched himself off the high porch in a diving tackle aimed at The Kid. The impact of the crash drove The Kid right out of the saddle and off the buckskin's back.

The two men fell heavily to the ground, causing the horses closest to them to dance around skittishly. The Kid knew he was in danger of being stepped on. Despite the fact that the fall had knocked the breath out of him, he brought the base of his right hand up sharply under the rough-neck's chin, driving the man's head back.

The Kid rolled away, heaved himself up on his

hands and knees, and dragged several deep breaths of air into his lungs.

His opponent, finding himself in just another brawl, recovered quickly. He threw himself at The Kid again, knocking him backward almost underneath the hooves of the nervous horses again.

"Give 'em room!" Culhane bellowed at the men with him. "Move those horses back!"

As the posse men reined their mounts back, the roughneck began slugging at The Kid, who was able to block only some of the blows. A couple times, a knobby fist slammed into his jaw as the man knelt on top of him.

The Kid shrugged off the punishment and shot his hands up, grabbing the front of the man's shirt. A powerful heave sent the roughneck flying over his head to go rolling in the dusty street.

The Kid rolled over and scrambled up, barely making it to his feet first. Quickly looking around, he had a fraction of a minute to see Culhane holding a gun on the second roughneck before the first man charged him again, arms windmilling as he threw wild punch after wild punch.

Ducking low, The Kid let the savage blows go over his head. He lunged forward, planting his head in the man's belly as he wrapped his arms around the man's thighs and heaved again. With a startled yell, the roughneck crashed down on his back with bone-jarring, tooth-rattling force.

The Kid levered himself up and drove a knee

into the man's belly. Their positions were reversed, and he didn't intend to waste his advantage. Moving his fists almost too fast to see, he smashed punch after punch into the man's face.

It didn't take long to knock all the fight out of him. The man's eyes swelled shut, and blood gushed from his flattened nose. He pawed feebly at The Kid and whimpered, "No more! No more!"

"Morgan!" Culhane's voice lashed out at The Kid. "That's enough, blast it! You're gonna kill him!"

"Better than letting him . . . kill me," The Kid said a little breathlessly as he stopped pounding his fists into the roughneck's face.

He heaved himself to his feet and left the man bleeding in the dirt as he looked around for his hat. The black Stetson lay a few feet away. It was dusty, but at least it hadn't been stepped on by any of the horses. He picked it up, slapped it against his leg to get some of the dust off, and settled it on his head.

His jaw ached where he'd been punched. He figured he would have a bruise there by the time the day was over.

The fight had drawn some of the citizens of Stubbtown out of the buildings. They stood around watching with avid interest. Just the arrival of the posse would have been enough to break the monotony of life in that wide place in the trail. A brawl on top of it was a bonus.

None of the townspeople seemed upset that The Kid had handed a beating to the roughneck. There was a good chance he and his friend had a history of bullying folks.

Culhane told the man still on the porch, "Take your pard and get out of here, mister. In case you didn't notice this badge on my shirt, I'm a Texas Ranger, and this is a legally appointed posse. Interferin' with a peace officer is against the law, and the two of you are lucky I don't arrest you. Now skedaddle!"

The man was only too happy to get out of it without a beating . . . or worse. He hurried down from the porch and went to his friend, grunting with effort as he lifted the groggy roughneck to his feet. Together, they stumbled toward the saloon.

Culhane holstered his gun. He motioned toward the store and told the other members of the posse, "All right, get in there and get what supplies you want. We ain't got all day."

The Kid got his buckskin and pack horse and tied their reins to the hitch rack in front of the store. He glanced up at the redheaded woman, who'd moved to the edge of the porch.

She said to Culhane, "Excuse me, sir. Did I hear you say that you're a Texas Ranger?"

Culhane raised a finger to the brim of his hat and nodded politely. "Yes, ma'am, that's right. Asa Culhane, by name."

"I'm Lucille Morrison," she said. "I want to thank you and your man there for stepping in to help me."

"Don't thank me," Culhane replied with a shake of his head. "Jumpin' into the middle of this ruckus was all Morgan's idea. Although I got to admit that I probably would have if he hadn't beat me to it, Miz Morrison."

"It's Miss Morrison," the redhead told him with a smile. "I'm not married. And that's the crux of the problem I find confronting me now."

Culhane frowned. "You said the crutch of the problem . . . ?"

"No, crux. The center. The very thing that's causing me trouble. That being the lack of a husband."

The Ranger shook his head. "I'm mighty sorry, ma'am, but I ain't followin' you at all. If you're lookin' for a husband among this bunch, you're out of luck. We're a posse, hot on the trail of a bunch of murderin' outlaws."

"But you seem to be heading toward San Antonio," the woman persisted.

"Well, yeah, in that general direction, right enough," Culhane admitted.

The redhead clutched her bag tighter and smiled. "Then it shouldn't be any problem for you to take me with you."

Culhane's eyebrows rose in shocked surprise. The Kid's face remained expressionless. He'd expected the woman to suggest something along those lines.

Culhane said, "I'm sorry, Miss Morrison, but I told you, we're after a mighty bad bunch of owlhoots. The last thing in the world you want to do is come along with us."

"But I have to get to San Antonio, and I don't think it would be safe for a woman to travel alone all that distance. When you find those badmen you're pursuing, I'll stay back, well out of the way. You won't be put to any trouble."

Culhane gave a stubborn shake of his head. "No, ma'am. It's a loco idea, and I won't do it."

"Then you mean to leave me stranded here in this terribly dreary place?"

Culhane looked like he was starting to get mad now. "Look, ma'am, I don't know how you came to be here—"

"I was abandoned here," the redhead broke in. "Lied to and then abandoned by an evil man."

A sort of understanding began to dawn in Culhane's eyes. "This hombre promised to marry you, did he?"

A flush spread over the woman's peaches-and-cream complexion. "That's right, and I believed him," she said in obvious embarrassment. "I traveled with him this far—it's scandalous, I know, but there's nothing I can do about that now—and then he stopped to sit in on a poker game at that saloon down the street. Fortune smiled on him, and he won a considerable amount of money. Our plan was to go to El Paso and open a store there, and I thought this windfall would make it easier for us. But then this morning"—her voice hardened—"I woke up and he was gone. So was our buggy."

"I'm sure sorry to hear about that, but I'm afraid it don't change anything. We don't have any spare horses, and even if we did"—Culhane smiled faintly—"you ain't exactly rigged out for ridin'."

"I have a little money," the redhead said. "I thought it might be wise to keep a little my so-called fiancé didn't know about." Her mouth twisted bitterly. "As it turns out, I was right. I can buy a horse of my own, along with a saddle and whatever gear I need. I just need the protection of a group of honorable men." She gave the Ranger a dazzling smile. "And it's obvious that's what I've found in you gentlemen."

Culhane took off his hat, ran a hand over his thinning hair, and grimaced as indecision warred inside him. He glanced at The Kid. "What do you think, Morgan?"

The Kid looked up intently at the woman for a long moment before saying, "I think Miss Morrison could use a helping hand. If she can keep up, I think we should take her along."

"Oh, I can keep up, Mister . . . Morgan, was it?" She gave him the same smile. "I assure you I won't be a hindrance."

Culhane clapped his hat back on his head. "No offense, ma'am, but you'd better not be. If you are, we'll leave you behind and you'll have to shift for yourself. And you ain't got much time to get ready to ride with us, either. We'll be pullin' out of this burg as soon as my men finish pickin' up some supplies. If you're gonna buy a horse
and an outfit, you'd better get busy."

"There's a livery stable down the street," The Kid said. "I'm still in good shape on supplies, so I'll give the lady a hand."

"I would appreciate that very much, Mr. Morgan." She started down the steps.

Culhane was still mounted. He swung down from the saddle and stepped aside to let the redhead pass. The Kid joined her, and as he did, Culhane said in a low voice, "Don't lose track o' time, Morgan."

"Don't worry," The Kid assured him. "I won't."

He fell in alongside the woman, and they walked toward the livery stable at the other end of the street. When they were out of earshot of Culhane, the redhead said, "Thanks for not giving me away, Kid."

"Don't thank me just yet," he snapped. "I might still tell Culhane the truth. It all depends on what explanation you have for that load of crap you just handed him, Lace."

152

CHAPTER 17

A low, throaty laugh came from her. "You saw through me right away, didn't you?"

"As soon as I laid eyes on you," The Kid said. "It hasn't been that long since I saw you, remember?"

"Almost a year."

The Kid shook his head. "That's not long enough." In fact, he was unlikely to *ever* forget Lace McCall. She had come close to killing him . . . and she had also saved his life.

And she was the only woman he'd made love with since Rebel's death.

Lace was a bounty hunter, and they had met in New Mexico Territory when there was a price on The Kid's head. She had intended to collect that bounty, but in the end she had helped him to clear his name.

She had been seriously wounded, and the last time he'd seen her, she had been recuperating from those injuries.

He had covered the cost of her medical care—Conrad Browning was a rich man, after all, whether The Kid still claimed that identity or not—and had provided money to make sure Lace's daughter back in Kansas City was taken care of properly.

But he hadn't been back to visit her. He had been consumed by a quest of his own. Since it had come to an end, he hadn't felt like seeing anybody from his past.

Fate had taken that decision out of his hands.

"I'll bet you can guess what I'm doing here," Lace said as they approached the livery stable.

"I suspect it has something to do with a man named Warren Latch. How big is the bounty on his head?"

"Ten thousand dollars. And the rewards on the other men I know are in his gang add up to several thousand more dollars, at the very least. Bringing them in would be a nice big haul for me, Kid."

He stopped walking, and so did she.

"I offered to take care of you—"

"The hell with that," she snapped, interrupting him. "I don't need anybody to take care of me. Men used to offer to do that when I was working in the whorehouse, and when I finally believed one of them, it didn't work out too well."

The Kid remembered the story she had told him in an isolated camp in New Mexico . . .

"I wasn't always a bounty hunter. My mama . . . she worked in a house in St. Louis. You know?"

"I know," The Kid said. "You don't have to tell me any of this if you don't want to."

"If I didn't want to, I wouldn't be telling

154

you," she snapped. Her tone softened again as she went on. "I was born there. She wanted a better life for me than she had, so she moved to Kansas City and tried to find a real job there. It was hard for her, though, and after a while . . . well, she went back to it. With all that, I don't guess anybody would be real surprised to hear I turned out the same way."

The Kid didn't say anything, although actually he was a little surprised.

"I wound up in a family way," she went on. "One of my customers, a man named McCall, offered to marry me. I took him up on it. I wanted my child to have a name. He turned out to be a pretty bad sort, though. He didn't treat me good. After a while I found out he was even worse than I thought. I happened to see a wanted poster with his picture on it. The man on the poster had a different name, but McCall was one of the names he was said to use sometimes. I went home, and the next time he raised his hand to me, I was ready. I shot the son of a bitch."

"You killed him?" The Kid asked.

"No, I just put a bullet in his knee, and while he was rolling around on the floor and screaming, I went and found a policeman and told him there was a wanted fugitive in my house. They hauled him off, and I claimed the reward. I got it, too. That was enough for me to *be able to set my mama and my little girl up so they'd be all right." She laughed. "That was how I found out I liked bounty hunting a lot better than I liked being a whore."*

"And that's what you've been doing for the past few years?"

"Five years," she said. "I already knew how to fight. I taught myself how to ride and shoot and found that I really took to it . . ."

That was putting it mildly. Lace was as good a shot as any man The Kid had ever seen with the exception of himself and his father, and she could sit a saddle all day without getting weary. He wouldn't count her out in a bare-knuckles brawl, either. She packed quite a punch.

But she'd also been packing some fairly serious bullet wounds the last time he'd seen her.

"The doctor said you probably wouldn't ever be in good enough shape to go back to bounty hunting."

Lace shrugged and shook her head. "I'm here, aren't I? Doctors don't know everything. I'm fine. Hell, I was laid up for so long I thought I'd go crazy. I feel a lot better now than I did when I was laying around doing nothing."

"Why the long, involved story you told Culhane about being abandoned here by some lothario?" The Kid asked.

Lace grinned as mischievous lights sparkled in

her green eyes. "Pretty convincing, wasn't it? I made it up on the spot to get that Texas Ranger to go along with what I wanted, once I realized I could get a whole posse to help me."

"Nobody here in Stubbtown knows any different?"

"How could they? I just rode in a little while ago." Lace laughed. "Stubbtown. What a horrible name. Would you want to admit you were from Stubbtown?"

"Probably not." The Kid had to admit it.

"I left my horses at the livery stable and changed into this getup." She gestured at the hat and traveling dress. "I planned to ask some questions about Latch, and thought I might be more likely to get honest answers if nobody knew I was hunting bounty. Now that's not necessary. You're on his trail, so I'll just come along with you and the posse."

She was a quick thinker, he had to give her credit for that.

"By the time anybody who lives here heard your story and started to question it, you'll be gone," he said.

"That's the idea." She gave him an intent look. "How about it, Kid? Is it going to work?"

"Do you know what Warren Latch did a few days ago?" he asked grimly. "Do you know what he's capable of?"

"Damn right I know," Lace said. "I have contacts at the Ranger post in San Antonio. When Culhane wired there about what happened at Fire Hill, I got wind of it. I knew they were headed in this direction. That's why I set out to intercept the gang somewhere along the way."

The Kid grunted. "One woman against a gang of forty killers."

"I thought I'd figure something out when the time came," she said with a smile. "And so I have. What I don't know is how Latch got past me."

"It's a big country," The Kid pointed out.

"Yeah, I guess so. And you still haven't answered my question, Kid. Do I get to come along . . . or are you going to tell Culhane the truth?"

"Even if I did, he might take you along. We've whittled down the odds a little, but Latch's bunch still outnumbers the posse by quite a bit. If I tell Culhane how good you are in a fight, he's liable to offer you a job as a temporary Texas Ranger!"

Lace shook her head. "No thanks. I want to be able to collect all the bounties I can."

They couldn't stand out there in the street much longer, The Kid realized. They had already been talking for several minutes, and Culhane was liable to start wondering what was going on.

"If Culhane decides you can't come along, you'll just find some other way of going after Latch, won't you?"

Lace smiled. "You know me, Kid."

"Yeah, I do." He started toward the stable again. "Come on."

"Thanks, Kid. I'll see to it you don't regret it."

Not sure what she meant by that, he wasn't sure he wanted to know. He didn't regret the things they had done, but he wasn't interested in any sort of long-term romance, either.

"Are you going to keep up this ridiculous masquerade as a spurned woman?" he asked as they walked side by side.

"I almost have to, don't I? At least for the time being."

"You mean until you capture Latch and can claim the ten grand?"

"That's exactly what I mean." Lace laughed. "Will you go along with that, Kid?"

"Why not? I just hope it doesn't backfire on you."

"I won't let it."

Life had a way of dealing harshly with the plans people made, though. The Kid knew that all too well.

Inside the shadowy stable, Lace opened her bag and slipped a coin to the Mexican hostler. "Thanks for taking care of my horses, Felipe. If you hear any odd stories about me, for all you know they're true, *comprende*?"

Felipe bobbed his head. "*Sí, señorita*. Though we have known each other only a short time, you have always been the soul of honesty with me."

"That's right," Lace said with a smile. "Kid, help me get these horses ready. I still have to go back to the store and see if I can buy a riding outfit. Wouldn't do for Lucille Morrison to gallivant around in boots, jeans, and a buckskin shirt, now would it?"

"Go tend to that," The Kid told her. "I'll saddle your horse and get your supplies back on the pack horse."

"That's mighty generous of you."

"Just trying to speed things up so we can get back on Latch's trail."

"Warren Latch?" Felipe asked as his eyes widened. He made the sign of the cross. "I have heard of that one. It is said he is very much like the Devil himself."

"That's not far wrong," The Kid said.

"Señorita, you should not have anything to do with a man such as this Latch," Felipe advised.

"I don't have any choice," Lace said. "He's got something I want."

"What is that, señorita?"

"His head," Lace said.

CHAPTER 18

When Lace emerged from Brennaman's Trading Post and Emporium a short time later, she had traded the green traveling outfit for a brown, divided riding skirt, a gray shirt, and a brown vest that matched the skirt. So did the flat-crowned Stetson she wore with the strap taut under her chin. On her feet were short riding boots.

The Kid was mounted on his buckskin by then, sitting the saddle in front of the store as he held the reins not only of his pack animal but also Lace's, along with her saddle mount. As he handed the reins over to her, she asked, "Where are the others?"

"They pulled out a few minutes ago," The Kid explained. "I told Culhane I'd wait for you and that we would catch up in a little bit."

She swung up easily into the saddle. "Let's go. We don't want to let them get too far ahead."

The Kid gestured at the rifle in Lace's saddle boot. "How are you going to explain a genteel lady like Lucille Morrison being able to use a Winchester?"

"I'll think of something. I always do, don't I?"

"That's true." As they turned away from the store and started riding along the street, The Kid went on, "Where's Max?"

The big, shaggy cur had been Lace's inseparable companion during the ruckus over in New Mexico Territory. She shrugged. "He's back in Kansas City with my mother and Linda Sue. It's a good thing for a kid to have a dog around, and besides, Max is getting a little too old to go traipsing around with me all over the frontier, chasing outlaws. He deserves some time to lay on the porch in the sun."

"Sounds good," The Kid said.

Lace shot a glance over at him. "That's not for us. People like us don't get that luxury, Kid. We'll never see those so-called golden years. We'll meet somebody who's faster or trickier or just plain meaner, and we'll end up in a shallow grave somewhere, or with the coyotes scattering our bones. Sorry if you hadn't figured that out by now, but that's the way things happen for people like us."

"You're probably—"

Before The Kid could finish his sentence, a man stepped out from the mouth of the alley they were passing, pointed a revolver at them, and started pulling the trigger.

The shots were so loud The Kid couldn't hear the slug whistle past his ear, only inches away, but he sensed it. By that time his Colt was in his hand, coming up so swiftly it was only a blur. The gun roared and bucked.

The man in the alley mouth twisted halfway

around as The Kid's bullet punched into the left side of his chest. He struggled to stay on his feet and bring his gun back around toward the two riders, but the bullet had ripped through his heart, pulping it. With a groan, the man dropped to his knees and toppled sideways.

It was the first chance The Kid had to get a good look at the man. He recognized the rough-neck he'd had the brawl with earlier. The man had a friend, he recalled—

"To your left!" Lace called.

She had pulled her rifle from its sheath, and the Winchester snapped to her shoulder with the same sort of speed The Kid had demonstrated with the Colt. The repeater cracked as The Kid turned his head. He heard another shot at the same time and saw dust spurt in the street just in front of the buckskin.

Across the street, the man who had been crouched on the roof of a building lurched to his feet and doubled over from the pain of the rifle round that had bored into his guts. He dropped his own Winchester and followed it, falling from the roof and turning over once in midair to come crashing down on his back.

He had gotten off one shot at The Kid and Lace, and the cost of it had been his life.

The Kid was out of the saddle in a flash. He told Lace, "Cover me. I'll check them."

He was relatively sure both bushwhackers were

dead, but a man who wasn't careful about such things all too often wound up a corpse himself.

A quick look confirmed what The Kid thought. Neither of the roughnecks would ever bully anyone again.

The shots had drawn plenty of attention, although the citizens of Stubbtown were looking out curiously from the relative safety of the buildings, not venturing into the street.

However, once the gunfire stopped and didn't resume for a minute or two, they began to emerge.

The Kid replaced the round he had fired from the Colt and slid the revolver back into leather. He looked up at Lace. "That was pretty good shooting. You got that Winchester out and working in a hurry."

She shrugged. "Not fast enough to keep that bastard from almost ventilating you."

"Close doesn't count," The Kid said with a smile. He looked over at a man who was approaching him.

"Are they both dead?" the townie asked.

"That's right," The Kid said. "Is there going to be trouble over this?"

The man shook his head. "I don't see why there would be. Rudy Tomlinson and Jake Rivers were first-class sons of bitches—beg your pardon for my language, ma'am—and nobody in town's gonna be sorry to see them dead. Some of the people they ran roughshod over would probably be glad to buy you a drink, in fact, to thank you."

"We don't have time for that," The Kid said. "Is there any law here?"

"Not a bit, not even a constable."

"Then there's nothing to keep us from riding on."

"Not a thing," the townsman agreed. "We'll put these two in cheap pine boxes and plant them. The whole town's liable to turn out to bid them good riddance."

"You do that." The Kid took hold of the buckskin's reins and swung up in the saddle. "We have to be riding."

"I never saw anybody get a gun out as fast as you did, mister," the man went on in obvious excitement. "And ma'am, I never would have believed a lady could shoot like that."

"Well, then, you're easily surprised," Lace told him. She turned her horse and added, "Let's go, Kid. I don't want that posse getting too far ahead of us."

The Kid knew what she meant. She didn't want the posse accidentally capturing Warren Latch and his gang before she got a chance to be in on it and claim the reward. Lifting a hand briefly in farewell to the townsman, The Kid sent the buckskin loping after Lace and her horses.

It took them half an hour of brisk riding to catch up to the posse. When they did, several of the men stared at Lace with surprised expressions.

She didn't look like the rough-and-tumble bounty hunter The Kid had first met in New Mexico Territory, but her appearance was considerably different than it had been when the posse men first laid eyes on her in Stubbtown.

The riders all paused as The Kid and Lace joined them. Culhane tugged on the brim of his Stetson. "Ma'am."

"Ranger Culhane," she replied. "Thank you again for allowing me to accompany you."

"Could be you were right about bein' able to keep up. From the way you rode up, I'd say this ain't your first time on a horse."

Lace smiled. "Indeed it's not. I grew up on a farm. You'll find that I won't hold you back."

What she told Culhane wasn't strictly true, The Kid reflected, since actually she had grown up in a whorehouse, but she was right about not holding them back. And when it came down to a fight with Latch's gang, Lace would be worth two or three of the posse men, at the very least.

Culhane allowed everyone to rest the horses for a few minutes, then the posse moved out again. As they rode at the head of the group, Culhane said quietly to The Kid, "I thought I heard a few shots, 'way back yonder about where that settlement is."

"You did," The Kid agreed. "Those hombres who were bothering Miss Morrison when we rode in took exception to having their needings handed

166

to them. They tried to settle the score by bush-whacking us as we rode out."

Culhane's eyes narrowed. "I reckon the fact that you two are here means there are two less troublemakers in Stubbtown."

"You reckon correct," The Kid said.

He felt eyes on him and glanced over his shoulder to see Nick Burton staring at him with open admiration. He hoped Nick wouldn't say anything about him being Kid Morgan, but he supposed it didn't really matter.

Nick's gaze moved from The Kid to Lace, and his eyes showed admiration there as well, although of a different sort. Nick wasn't the only member of the posse she affected like that, The Kid thought with a faint, amused smile as he faced forward again. Lace wasn't the prettiest woman he had ever seen, but she was one of the most compelling.

"You didn't leave Reilly back there at the settlement like you said you were going to," The Kid commented quietly to Culhane.

"I thought about it," the Ranger said. "But I asked around, and there ain't no sawbones back there, so there didn't seem to be any point to makin' him stay. He would have put up a fuss about it, anyway."

The Kid knew that was true. He looked at Reilly, who was riding beside Abel Gustaffson.

The hatred radiating from both men was so

strong he could almost see it in the air around them.

It didn't take long for the posse to reach more rugged terrain. The wooded hills were small starting out, barely worthy of being called hills, but The Kid found them a refreshing change from the miles and miles of flat, mesquite-dotted prairie. The sun still beat down hotly, but somehow the presence of more green vegetation made the air seem slightly cooler.

"We ain't that far from San Antone now," Culhane commented late that afternoon. The Kid noticed a worried edge had crept into the Ranger's voice. "We need to catch up to Latch before he and his gang get to Bexar. If we don't, they're liable to split up and we won't ever be able to track 'em down." Culhane glanced over his shoulder at the posse and added quietly, "This bunch has already held together for longer than I thought they would."

"You can try pushing them harder," The Kid said. "Like you told me before, they'll stick. Too many of them have personal scores to settle with Latch for them not to."

"Yeah, you're probably right about that," Culhane said. "But the trail's gettin' harder to follow now that we're in these hills. That'll work against us."

The Kid knew he was right about that.

A short time later, the situation became more

difficult when the terrain suddenly got more rugged without any warning. The ground dropped into a deep, narrow canyon with steep hills on both sides. The slopes were covered thickly with cedars and junipers.

Culhane reined in and signaled a halt. As the posse came to a stop, the Ranger leaned forward in his saddle and frowned. "I don't much like the looks of this place," he said to The Kid, "but the trail leads down into that canyon."

Trampled grass and broken branches on some of the bushes testified that a large group of riders had passed through there in the fairly recent past.

Lace rode up alongside them. "They're less than a day ahead of us."

Culhane shot her a narrow-eyed look. "And how would you know that, ma'am?"

The Kid could tell by the look on her face she knew she had made a mistake. He could practically see the wheels of her brain spinning as she tried to come up with an answer.

"I told you my father was a farmer," she said. "What I didn't mention was that before he married my mother and took up farming, he did some scouting for the army. He taught me quite a bit. I guess you could say I was a tomboy back then."

"Uh-huh." It was obvious Culhane wasn't sure whether to believe her, but he didn't seem too suspicious as he went on, "Well, ma'am, you're right about those outlaws bein' less than a day ahead of us. I hope you're ready for some hard ridin', because we'll be pushin' on until it's too dark to see."

"That's fine with me, Mr. Culhane," she replied with a smile. "The sooner I get back to San Antonio, the better."

The Ranger turned in his saddle to address the posse. "The trail leads down into the canyon. We're gonna follow it, but keep your eyes peeled. This is a good spot for an ambush."

He waved the men forward. The Kid drew his Winchester from its saddle boot, and noticed that Lace did the same. Nick Burton and some of the other men followed their example.

Nick moved his horse alongside Lace's as the posse descended into the narrow canyon. He nodded toward the rifle she held. "Do you know how to use that, ma'am?"

She gave him an indulgent smile. "I've shot a rifle before, Mister . . . ?"

"Burton, ma'am, Nick Burton. But you should call me Nick. Mr. Burton's my pa. Or my grandpa, although folks usually call him Old Man Burton, on account of he's had a big ranch north of Fire Hill for so long. Well . . . where Fire Hill used to be, I guess you'd have to say."

The Kid and Culhane were riding in front of Lace and the youngster. As The Kid listened to Nick babbling on, he thought that was one more indication of just how smitten with her the young man was.

There was no telling how long Nick might have gone on, but at that moment he was rudely interrupted by the crack of a shot. The flat *whap!* of a bullet passing close by The Kid's head and Nick's cry of pain sounded together.

CHAPTER 19

"Spread out!" Culhane bellowed as members of the posse began to yell in alarm.

The Kid hadn't seen a muzzle flash or puff of gunsmoke to mark the bushwhacker's location, but he aimed at the sound of the shot anyway as he brought the Winchester to his shoulder and rapidly cranked off three rounds in that direction.

He twisted in the saddle and looked back to see Nick slumped over but still mounted. Lace had hold of his arm, supporting him.

"Get him to cover!" The Kid barked as more shots began to ring out from both slopes.

They had ridden into a trap, all right, and they would be lucky if any of them got out of it alive.

Hoping the pack horse would stay out of the line of fire, The Kid let go of the animal's reins and hauled the buckskin around.

Lace had grabbed Nick's reins when the young man dropped them, and led his horse as she galloped toward the nearest trees. The Kid sent the buckskin pounding after them.

Several members of the posse were down, and some who were still mounted might be wounded. He didn't yet know how badly Nick was hit, but was glad to see Culhane disappearing into some boulders on the other side of the canyon. The lawman seemed to be all right, as far as The Kid could tell.

More slugs whipped through the branches of the junipers and thudded into tree trunks as The Kid rode into the growth. He dismounted rapidly, taking his Winchester with him, and ducked behind one of the trees where he could see across the canyon to the opposite slope.

He couldn't do anything about the hidden rifleman on his side of the canyon, but he could make things hot for the varmints on the other side.

Thrusting the Winchester around the trunk, he opened fire, peppering the opposite slope with slugs as he rapidly worked the rifle's lever. The trees and the thick brush made it impossible for him to see what he was shooting at, but he hoped some of the bullets came close enough to make the bushwhackers jump.

After that initial volley, The Kid held his fire and took a moment to study the situation.

The posse had scattered the way Culhane ordered. They were spread out and fighting back, but were outnumbered. Two posse men lay unmoving where The Kid could see them. He knew they were either dead or badly wounded.

The ambushers had the advantage of the high ground and continued their barrage of gunfire.

Noise behind him in the brush made The Kid spin around with his finger on the Winchester's trigger, but he held his fire as Lace emerged from the growth.

"Hold on, Kid, it's just me," she said.

"I can see that. You know how close I came to shooting you?"

She flashed him a grin. "I trust your reflexes. I've seen them in action often enough."

He grunted as she moved to take cover behind a tree next to the one where he crouched. "How's Nick doing? I couldn't tell how bad he was hit."

"He's in quite a bit of pain," Lace said, "but I'm pretty sure he'll be all right. The bullet knocked a chunk of meat out of his left arm but didn't break the bone. I gave him a couple swigs from the flask I carry in my saddlebags and left him up there in the trees with the horses. He'll be fine."

"Until those bushwhackers higher up start working their way down toward us," The Kid pointed out.

Lace frowned. "I didn't think about that," she admitted. "I wanted to make sure you weren't hurt."

"We can stay here and shoot at those men on the other side of the canyon all day without knowing if we're doing any good," The Kid said. "I think it would be a better use of our time to start up this slope and see what we can find."

"Carve down the odds one at a time, you mean?" Lace asked. "I like that idea. Come on."

Bullets still whispered through the branches, but the outlaws were firing blindly just like the posse. The Kid didn't worry too much about those stray shots. If one of them found him, he would consider that his fate . . . assuming he lived long enough to think anything.

In the meantime, he was going to do his best to take the fight to the enemy.

He had no doubt the bushwhackers were some of Warren Latch's men. He didn't think a small group of would-be robbers would have attacked a bunch as large as the posse. It could be the entire gang, for all he knew. Nobody else would have a reason to bushwhack them.

Like a phantom, The Kid moved through the trees, using every available bit of cover so the riflemen on the other side of the canyon wouldn't spot him.

A few yards away, Lace was doing the same thing. The smile was gone from her face, replaced by an expression of grim determination.

They came to the place where she had left Nick Burton. The young man was slumped motionless on his side against a fallen tree.

For a second The Kid thought Lace had underestimated the seriousness of Nick's injuries and the young man had bled to death.

Then a loud snore came from Nick. He hadn't died or passed out. He had fallen asleep, even with gunshots going off all over the canyon.

The youngster must not have had much to drink in his life, The Kid thought with a smile, if two swigs of whiskey from Lace's flask had knocked him out like that.

Lace had torn a strip from Nick's shirt and bound up the wound on his arm. The cloth was bloodstained, but the bullet hole didn't seem to be bleeding a lot. He ought to be all right there, The Kid thought.

Nodding to Lace, he gestured to indicate they should continue to move on up the slope. The gunfire continued, and The Kid used the sound of the shots coming from above as a guide. He and Lace steered toward the blasts.

The reports got louder. Holding out a hand, he motioned for Lace to get down. They crouched behind trees.

The Kid studied the slope. After a minute or two, he spotted the barrel of a rifle poking out from some brush.

It was tempting to empty his Winchester into the bushes, but since it was possible another member of the posse had worked his way up there, just as The Kid and Lace had done, they needed to make sure who was in there.

Using hand signals, The Kid told Lace to stay where she was while he worked his way around behind the hidden rifleman. She didn't look very happy about that, but after a moment she gave him a grudging nod.

The Kid darted from tree to tree and finally had to go to his belly and crawl up the slope to remain unseen as he circled the brush. It took him several minutes to reach a position where he could see the man hidden there. The rifleman wasn't one of the posse men. He was a roughly dressed hombre with a short, ginger-colored beard, and he had an ugly grin on his face as he fired another shot into the canyon.

The Kid drew a bead on him and squeezed the trigger.

The crack of the Winchester was lost in all the other shots filling the canyon. The bearded man's head jerked to the side as the bullet from The Kid's rifle bored through it. He dropped his gun and fell bonelessly to the ground, rolling over a couple times before he came to a stop out in the open.

Lace saw the body and hurried forward. She paused long enough to pull the dead outlaw's revolver from its holster and tuck it behind her belt. She left the rifle where the man had dropped it.

"You need more armament?" The Kid asked dryly as Lace rejoined him.

"In my business, you can never have too many guns."

He supposed that was true. With a jerk of his chin, he indicated they should move on up the slope.

They stayed about ten yards apart. Lace had paused and was kneeling behind a boulder when a man suddenly came around it. He stopped short in obvious surprise when he saw her, but that lasted only a split second before he swung his rifle toward her with blinding speed.

The Kid saw that from the corner of his eye, but there was nothing he could do about it. Lace was between him and the gunman, and he couldn't take a shot at the man without running too great a risk of hitting her instead.

Lace was hardly defenseless, though. She threw herself to the ground as the outlaw fired, pulling the revolver from her belt as she did so. The man's shot went over her head, and from her angle she pumped a .45 slug up into his belly.

The man doubled over and fell, tumbling down the slope out of control as he screamed from the pain of being gut-shot.

By the time he came to a stop, Lace had twisted around and was ready to fire again. She drilled a slug through his head, putting him out of his misery.

That made two of Latch's men down. Lace gave The Kid a grim nod to let him know she was all right, and they resumed stalking their enemies.

The outlaws weren't the only danger. A bullet suddenly came from behind The Kid and thudded into the trunk of a nearby tree, scattering chips of bark.

He knew that shot had been fired by one of the men in the posse down below. They weren't aware he and Lace were up on the slope, working their way among the outlaws, and running the risk of being shot by one of their own allies.

The slope leveled out into a small shoulder of ground thrusting out from the canyon wall. The Kid heard the nervous whickering of horses. He and Lace had stumbled onto the spot where some of the bushwhackers' mounts were being held. It was bound to put a crimp in the outlaws' plans if they could stampede those animals, he thought with a faint smile. He motioned to Lace for her to go one way while he went the other.

They circled through the brush. The Kid heard horses moving around close by and crouched to part some branches and peer through the narrow gap. He saw a dozen horses in a clearing. Two of Latch's men were there with them.

The Kid looked across the clearing and spotted Lace peering through a tiny opening in the brush on that side. He caught her eye and pointed to himself, then to one of the outlaws. She nodded in understanding that The Kid would take that man and she would take the other.

As soon as both of Latch's men were dead, it would be simple to stampede the horses.

At that moment Lace let out a startled cry and came flying out of the brush with such force she lost her balance and sprawled on her face.

A man stepped into view behind her and planted a big, booted foot in the middle of her back to pin her to the ground. "Look what we have here, amigos."

CHAPTER 20

The man was a burly Mexican, and stealthier than he looked or he never would have been able to sneak up on Lace undetected like he had.

Of course, with all the shooting going on in the canyon, plus the sounds of the horses moving around, there was quite a bit of racket, which helped explain how she had been caught unaware.

Even with the man pinning her down with his foot, Lace continued to struggle. She had dropped her rifle, but The Kid could tell she was trying to reach the revolver she had taken from the dead man earlier.

The outlaw's jovial attitude disappeared as he rested the muzzle of the rifle he held one-handed against the back of her neck. "Stop fighting, señorita. I don't know what you're doin' out here, but you're in a bad spot."

"What are we gonna do with her, Ortiz?" one of the other men asked.

Ortiz leered down at Lace, who had ceased her struggles when she felt the cold, octagonal barrel of the Winchester pressing against her skin. "I don't know about you, Ramsey, but I can think of a few things I'd like to do with this one."

A third man shook his head dubiously. "I don't think Latch and Duval would be happy about that. We're supposed to be wiping out that posse, not sporting with some gal that happened along."

"Happened along?" Ortiz repeated. "This little hellcat did not just happen along, amigo. She was carrying a rifle, and the way she was trying to get to her belt, she must have a pistol there as well. No, I think she is part of the posse."

"A woman, riding with a posse? I never heard of such a thing!"

Lace spoke up. "You'd better let me go. You're going to be in big trouble if you don't." Her voice showed the strain of being held down like she was.

Ortiz boomed out a laugh. "We're going to be in big trouble, señorita? How do you figure that?"

"Somebody will come to help me!"

"You think so? Really?" Ortiz took off his sombrero and lifted it mockingly above his head. "Here, I make it easy for them. I am a good target, eh?"

He certainly was. The Kid could have put a

bullet in the man's head at any time during the past few minutes.

But he had held his fire because of the rifle Ortiz had pointed at Lace. The Kid felt certain there was a cartridge in the chamber, just waiting for a squeeze of Ortiz's finger on the trigger.

If that rifle went off, the bullet would probably sever Lace's spine . . . if it didn't ricochet, range up into her brain, and kill her instantly. That would be a kinder fate than lying there paralyzed while she slowly bled to death.

But The Kid couldn't just crouch there in the brush and do nothing. Carefully, he slid the Winchester's barrel through the gap in the branches and settled the stock against his shoulder. His cheek rested against the smooth wood as he peered over the sights.

Ortiz clapped the sombrero back on his head and laughed. "It seems no one is coming to help you after all, señorita. So unless you want the next few minutes to become very unpleasant, you should tell me who you are, what you are doing here, and where your companions are."

"Go to hell!" Lace said. "That's all I'll tell you!"

"I think not, señorita." Ortiz's foot came down harder on her back. Lace's head turned to the side, and The Kid could see how her face was twisted in pain. "You are the one who will soon believe you are in hell."

The Kid took a deep breath and settled the

sights of his rifle on the barrel of Ortiz's rifle. It was a lot smaller target than the man's bulky body, but the only chance he had of saving Lace.

The shot carried with it a risk of its own. Even if he hit the outlaw's rifle, the slug could ricochet and strike Lace. It was a chance he had to take.

The Kid squeezed the trigger.

The rifle cracked and bucked against his shoulder. With a loud *spang!,* the bullet hit Ortiz's rifle and knocked it out of the startled outlaw's hands.

Ortiz was so surprised he took a step back, and that was his undoing.

As soon as the weight on her back was gone, Lace rolled over and plucked the Colt from behind her belt with flashing speed. The gun roared as she fired shot after shot into Ortiz's groin and belly.

At the same time, The Kid levered his rifle, swung it to the side, and fired again. One of the other two outlaws flung his hands in the air and died without a sound as he slid to the ground.

The third man didn't stay to put up a fight. He ducked behind the horses, evidently hoping they would shield him.

That proved to be a mistake. The Kid put three fast shots into the ground near the already-nervous horses, and that was all it took to make them bolt.

The third outlaw let out a panic-stricken screech

as the animals ran into him, knocking him off his feet. His scream ended abruptly as the horses stampeded right over him, their steel-shod hooves pounding him into a gory mess.

The Kid burst out of the brush and ran toward Lace.

Ortiz had crumpled, lying on his side, curled around the bullet holes Lace had put in him. He was still alive. Tears of agony welled from his eyes and coursed down his dusty face as he lifted his head to look at Lace, who had climbed to her feet and stood over him.

"You should have listened to me, you stupid bastard," she said as she pointed the Colt at him.

The outlaw's eyes rolled up in their sockets and his head flopped back to the ground before she could pull the trigger.

"You'd be wasting a bullet," The Kid told her as he came up to her. "He's already dead."

"Yeah, well, I'm not sure it would have been a waste to wipe that smirk off his face for good." Lace lowered the pistol.

"I think it's gone. All those slugs you put in his belly took care of that."

"He had it coming. Sneaking up on me like that and kicking me in the back."

"I'm surprised you didn't hear him."

Lace glared at The Kid but didn't say anything. Ortiz had gotten the drop on her, and nothing she could say would change that.

The Kid turned to survey the bench where the horses had been held. They were gone now, pulled loose from their pickets and vanished into the trees. Their owners would be in for a surprise.

Lace took some fresh cartridges from a pocket in her riding skirt and began thumbing them into the Colt's cylinder.

The Kid smiled. "You always carry extra ammunition with you?"

Lace snapped the revolver's cylinder closed and looked up at him. "Doesn't everyone?"

She had a point there. His Winchester was starting to run a little low, so he reloaded it, too, pushing the shells in through the loading gate.

"Do we keep moving?" Lace asked.

The Kid nodded. "There were about a dozen horses here. We've accounted for five men."

"Almost half."

"But still plenty of work to do," he said. "There are some boulders a couple hundred yards farther on. I caught a glimpse of them through the trees. That looked like a good spot for some of Latch's men to fort up."

"So what do we do, waltz up there and knock?"

"We'll figure that out when we get there," The Kid told her. "Isn't that what you always say?"

"Yeah, yeah, let's go."

They left the dead outlaws behind and started moving along the slope again. They were a good distance from Nick Burton, and The Kid hoped the young man was all right. With any luck, Nick would sleep through the rest of the battle.

The Kid's thoughts turned to strategy. He had a hunch Warren Latch had split his forces, leaving a group to ambush the posse while the rest of the outlaws forged on toward San Antonio. Judging from the amount of gunfire coming from both sides of the canyon, The Kid guessed about half of the gang had been left behind. If the posse could stay hunkered down and hold out for a while without losing too many men, while he and Lace hunted up on the slope like beasts of prey, they could do some significant damage to Latch's gang. That would make the odds closer to even when the posse finally caught up to the rest of the outlaws, he thought.

Assuming they did before Latch and the others reached the sprawling city of San Antonio.

The Kid and Lace came in sight of the boulders scattered along the slope. A haze of gunsmoke hung in the air over the rocks, telling The Kid some of Latch's men were hidden there, just as he'd suspected. He saw several spurts of flame from the barrels of rifles thrust out from behind the boulders.

"We need to get above them," he told Lace as they paused to assess the situation.

"How?" she asked. "There's too much open ground between here and those rocks, all the way to the top of the slope."

"We'll have to circle around far enough that they can't see us."

"If they're smart, they'll have posted a guard or two just to keep an eye on their backs."

"Then we'll have to find those guards and deal with them." The Kid pointed to some smaller boulders higher up on the slope. "You know, if we could start some of those rocks rolling . . ."

Lace grinned. "We could dump a nice little avalanche right on top of those outlaws."

"That's what I was thinking." The Kid nodded. "Let's go."

Staying in the trees, they began working their way higher. The slope became so steep they had to drop to all fours and pull themselves up by grasping branches and roots. Even in the shade of the trees, the day was hot. The Kid was soon drenched in sweat.

"Did you see how many in the posse were hit in the first volley?" Lace asked.

"I know at least two men were down," he replied. "I wouldn't be surprised if there were more."

"We're whittling down Latch's bunch, but they're doing the same to us. What about the Ranger?"

"Culhane? I saw him make it to some rocks. He seemed to be all right."

"Good. I don't like the looks of some of the rest of those men." Lace shuddered a little. "Especially the one who's all bandaged up. He makes me nervous, Kid."

The Kid thought about how Vint Reilly had killed the Gustaffsons' dog. "I don't think he's right in the head anymore. He's got good reason to be a little loco. His wife was killed when Latch's gang raided Fire Hill, and he got those burns when he was trapped in his house while it was burning down around him."

"I'm sorry about all that, but I still don't like him."

"Neither do I," The Kid admitted. "But as long as Culhane's around, he'll ride herd on Reilly and the others."

"Yeah, but what if something happens to him?"

"Then he's expecting me to take charge of the posse."

Lace stopped climbing and looked over at him. "Kid Morgan, the man who was wanted by the law all over New Mexico and Arizona Territories?"

"Culhane doesn't know I'm that Morgan. Anyway, those were trumped-up charges, and you know it."

"Yeah, but you've still had more experience running from posses than you've had leading them."

That was true. "Let's hope it doesn't come to that. I don't want the job."

They started climbing again, and reached the canyon rim a few minutes later. It was rugged and rocky, and in several places the slope turned abruptly into a sheer bluff reaching up into the blue Texas sky.

A little brush grew along the base of those bluffs, providing some cover as they worked their way behind the boulders Latch's men were using as a stronghold.

No one challenged The Kid and Lace as they reached the small boulders they intended to push down the slope, starting a rock slide that would create havoc among the outlaws. Some of Latch's men might be killed in the slide, and the chaos would give The Kid and Lace a chance to pick off the others.

That was their hope, anyway.

The Kid studied the men behind the rocks about a hundred yards below them. He could see quite a few of the outlaws from where he was, but if he and Lace started shooting, Latch's men would turn around and open fire on them. The avalanche idea was better.

And if it worked, they could start bringing down some of the riflemen on the other side of the canyon.

The Kid pointed to one of the rocks. "That one. If I can start it moving, it'll topple down and take several more with it. Once they're rolling, the slide will develop quickly."

"Then we'll both push," Lace said. "You know I'm strong, Kid."

He knew that, but he also knew she had been

seriously wounded less than a year earlier. Too much heaving and straining might damage something inside her.

"I can do it." He set his rifle down.

"Are you going to argue with me at a time like this?"

"When do we not argue?" he muttered.

"Well, I remember one night on the trail—"

"Never mind. You can help me. Just don't hurt yourself."

"Don't worry about that. Those outlaws are the ones I want to hurt."

She put her rifle on the ground, too, and joined him behind the boulder he had picked out. It was about four feet tall and massive. The Kid knew he couldn't have budged it even an inch if it had been sitting on level ground.

Luckily the boulder was on a fairly steep slope. All they had to do was start rocking it a little. Once they did, it shouldn't take very long to dislodge it and get it rolling and bounding down toward the bushwhackers.

"Put your shoulder into it." The Kid leaned down and got his own shoulder wedged against the rough stone. Close beside him, Lace got into position, too.

"I'm ready, Kid," she said through gritted teeth.

"All right, when I give the word—"

At that instant a bullet whistled between their heads, hit the boulder, and ricocheted off with a high-pitched whine.

CHAPTER 21

The Kid's head jerked around as he peered up at the bluff looming above them.

About forty feet above their heads was a small ledge he hadn't noticed earlier. A man knelt on that ledge with a rifle in his hands. The rifle cracked again.

Once more The Kid felt the heat of a bullet passing close by his head and heard the whine as it ricocheted off the boulder.

The man must have climbed up there to keep an eye on his fellow outlaws down below. The Kid had suspected there might be a guard, but he and Lace hadn't run into any sentries.

Until now.

Instinct brought his Colt out with blinding speed, but Lace was almost as fast beside him. Her gun began to boom as she said, "I'll cover you, Kid! Roll that rock!"

He saw the rifleman on the ledge duck back hurriedly as Lace's slugs smacked into the sandstone bluff around him and sent puffs of dust and chunks of rock flying into the air.

The Kid holstered his Colt and turned back to the boulder. They didn't have much time. The other outlaws were bound to hear the firing behind them and realize some sort of threat was back there.

Planting his feet, The Kid put his shoulder against the rock and heaved with all the strength he could muster.

The rock didn't go anywhere.

He gritted his teeth and threw his weight against the boulder again.

Beside him, the hammer of Lace's revolver fell on an empty chamber with a resounding click. "I'm out!"

"Grab my gun!" The Kid yelled to her as he heaved against the boulder for a third time. He felt the weight of his Colt leave the holster as Lace followed his command.

The brief respite had given the outlaw on the ledge a chance to risk another shot, and the man's rifle cracked again. The Kid felt the fiery kiss of a slug nicking his arm before it hit the boulder and screamed off into the distance. That arm and shoulder went numb for an instant as he slumped against the rock.

"Kid!" Lace cried out in alarm.

"I'm all right." He gritted his teeth.

Sensation came flooding back into his arm, bringing with it pain. He focused on that pain, drew it to him, embraced it, and took strength from the anger it caused to well up inside him.

"Roll, damn you!" he yelled as he summoned all the strength he had left and heaved against the boulder one last time.

With a grating of stone against stone, it moved.

And just as The Kid had suspected, that was all it took. Suddenly overbalanced, the boulder tipped forward, and went over with a crash and a roar. The Kid lost his balance, too, and fell as the massive rock toppled away from him.

The blood was pounding so hard in his head he couldn't hear much of anything else. But he was aware of Lace grabbing his collar and hauling him to his feet.

"We have to pull back!" she shouted at him.

The Kid realized why as he saw bullets smacking into the bluff around them. The outlaws in the rocks below had turned around and were blazing away at the two of them.

The attack didn't last but a moment. Latch's men suddenly had a much bigger threat than The Kid and Lace to deal with. The boulder he had dislodged struck another rock and started it rolling, then another and another as the slide spread out and rumbled down the slope.

The Kid and Lace threw themselves behind some brush and watched as dust billowed into the air from the falling rocks. They couldn't see the outlaws below anymore, but even over the racket of the rock slide, they heard screams from the men who were caught in its path.

A bullet sliced through the branches near them. The man on the ledge above was still firing at them, but now that they had moved he didn't have a very good angle.

Lace said, "If I could just get my hands on my rifle . . ."

Both Winchesters were lying where their owners couldn't get to them without exposing themselves to the fire from the man on the ledge.

The Kid put a hand on Lace's shoulder. "Wait. There's no use risking your life. If we stay right here, he can't hit us."

She turned her head to look at him. "Speaking of that, how bad are you hit, Kid?"

He looked down at his upper left arm. Blood stained his sleeve, but not a lot of it. He reached inside his shirt and carefully explored the wound with his fingers, wincing as he did so. "I'll be all right. It's barely a scratch. Hurt like blazes for a minute, but it's already better. I can use my arm with no trouble."

"You were lucky."

"I know."

Luck was one thing that seemed to follow him. He'd had more than his share of it . . . both good and bad.

Lace handed The Kid's gun back to him and reloaded her revolver. The rumble was fading below them as the avalanche played out. Dust still filled the air, so they couldn't see if any of the outlaws had survived.

The Kid's hand tightened around the Colt's grip. If any of Latch's men were still alive, he and Lace would soon have a fight on their hands.

As the dust cleared, several men on horseback emerged from some trees farther downslope. The Kid recognized Asa Culhane in the lead. The Gustaffsons, Thad and Bill, were with him.

The Kid wasn't the only one who saw the men from the posse. The outlaw on the ledge spotted them, too, and opened fire.

While the man was distracted, The Kid rolled out into the open and grabbed his rifle. He came up on a knee, lifted the repeater to his shoulder, and fired twice as he aimed up at the ledge.

The outlaw cried out as the bullets ripped through him. He dropped his Winchester and fell, landing with his head and one arm hung limply over the edge.

Lace dashed out from cover and grabbed up her rifle as well. She whirled toward the boulders where the other outlaws had been hidden.

No shots came from down there. The avalanche had wiped the area clean, succeeding beyond what The Kid had hoped. He saw several huddled, gory shapes that had once been men, but that was all.

"Morgan!" Culhane shouted. "Morgan, is that you?"

The Kid lifted his rifle above his head and waved it back and forth a couple times in a signal for the Ranger and his companions to come ahead.

When Culhane and the Gustaffson boys rode up to them, Culhane stared at Lace and exclaimed,

"Good Lord, Miss Morrison, were you right in the middle of this ruckus?"

"Circumstances left me no choice, Mr. Culhane," she told him.

"I reckon not. I reckon you weren't lyin' when you said you knew how to shoot, too." Culhane turned to The Kid and nodded to the blood-stained shirt sleeve. "How bad are you hit?"

"It's nothing to worry about," The Kid assured him. "What about the rest of the men?"

A few shots still rang out from the other side of the canyon. The outlaws over there hadn't given up, but it sounded like they were having trouble finding targets.

"I don't know," Culhane said in reply to The Kid's question. "They're scattered all to hell and gone, up and down this canyon. Looked like we lost at least a couple men, but other than that, I ain't sure."

The Kid nodded. Culhane's assessment agreed with his.

A bullet suddenly whined overhead.

"Those varmints on the other side are tryin' to get the range on us," Culhane went on. "We'd better hunt some cover."

The Ranger was right. The Kid knew they were in range of the riflemen on the other side of the canyon. Although it would be a long shot from there, long shots sometimes found their targets.

"Climb up behind me, ma'am," Culhane

offered, taking his left foot out of the stirrup so Lace could mount. He grasped her hand and helped her swing up behind him.

"You can ride with me," Thad told The Kid, who accepted the invitation. The five of them rode quickly back into the trees so the gunmen on the other side of the canyon couldn't see them.

Safely hidden, they dismounted.

Culhane took his hat off and shook his head in seeming amazement. "It looks to me like the two of you wiped out the whole bunch on this side. How in the world did you do it?"

"We were lucky," The Kid replied, repeating what Lace had said a few minutes earlier.

Culhane grunted. "Lucky . . . and mighty good shots, I'd say. I don't reckon I've ever seen the like. When I heard all them rocks tumblin' down, I knew somethin' was goin' on, so I figured I'd better check it out." Culhane nodded toward the Gustaffsons. "Ran into these two boys on the way up here. They had the same idea."

"And we were looking for Nick, too," Thad said. "Have you seen him?"

The Kid nodded. "He's all right. He got winged in that opening volley, but Miss Morrison tended to him." He pointed. "We left him in the trees, a couple hundred yards back that way."

"It might be a good idea if we went back to make sure nothing else happened to him," Lace suggested.

Culhane agreed. "Let's go."

Leading the horses, they started through the woods. Sporadic gunfire still popped and banged.

The ambush had turned into a standoff.

Reaching the spot where they had left Nick Burton, The Kid saw with alarm that the young man was gone.

"Is this the right place?" Lace asked as she frowned worriedly. "I would have sworn that was the log where he was lying. I gave him some whiskey to dull the pain of being wounded, and he sort of . . . passed out."

"This is the place," The Kid said. "He's got to be around here some—"

A sudden crackle of brush behind them was followed by a man's harsh voice ordering, "Don't move!"

Swinging around anyway, the five of them froze at the sight of an outlaw standing there, one arm locked cruelly around Nick's throat holding him up while the other hand pressed the barrel of a revolver against the youngster's head.

Chapter 22

"Take it easy, mister," Culhane said. "You got to know if you kill that boy, you won't make it outta here alive."

"Neither will he," the gunman said. "And some

of you may not, either. Just give me one of those horses, and I'll light a shuck out of here. I'll let the boy go when I'm out of range."

Culhane shook his head. "Can't do it. I'm sworn to uphold the law, and that don't include lettin' a wanted outlaw ride away, hostage or no hostage."

The man's eyes widened in disbelief and anger. "Are you loco?" he demanded. "I'll kill this little bastard! I swear I will!"

"Don't . . . don't listen to him . . . Ranger," Nick croaked, forcing the words past the arm across his throat. "Go ahead and . . . shoot him!"

The outlaw looked at Nick and snarled, "Why, you little—"

As soon as the man was distracted, The Kid's hand came up, moving too fast for the eye to follow. His gun blasted, and the outlaw's head snapped back sharply as the bullet bored through his brain and exploded out the back of his skull.

The slug's impact sent the man flying backward, arms outflung. His gun sailed out of his hand, unfired. With a heavy thud, the dead outlaw landed on his back.

Bill Gustaffson let out a whistle of admiration. "That was *some* shootin'!" he exclaimed.

The Kid had faced a similar situation a short time earlier, when Ortiz had been threatening Lace with his rifle. He didn't shoot then.

This time, close enough to the outlaw, The Kid was confident he could make the shot and kill the outlaw instantly, before the man could pull the trigger.

And that was how it had worked out, happening so fast Nick was left standing there, his eyes open wide, remaining motionless for a couple seconds as if the outlaw were still holding the gun on him.

"Ohhhh." Nick's knees buckled, and he fell to the ground.

Thad and Bill sprang forward to help him.

Culhane looked over at The Kid through eyes gone narrow with suspicion. "I'm startin' to think you're some sort of gunslinger, Morgan. You sure there ain't no wanted posters out on you?"

"I'm positive," The Kid said as he replaced the spent round in his Colt. He didn't look at Lace, thinking she might be grinning.

Culhane didn't look convinced, but he didn't press the issue. He turned to the Gustaffsons, who were kneeling on either side of Nick. "Is he all right?"

"I think he just fainted," Thad said.

"I might faint, too, if a bullet came as close to my ear as that one had to come to his," Bill added.

"Let's get him sitting up."

The brothers lifted Nick into a sitting position, and Thad started slapping his face lightly to bring him around.

Culhane turned to look in the direction of the gunmen on the other side of the canyon. "Most of the posse's still pinned down. You reckon there's any chance we can get over there and do to that bunch what you did to the varmints over here?"

"I doubt if we'll find boulders we can use to start another avalanche," The Kid said. "That would be asking for too much luck."

Culhane rubbed his jaw and nodded. "Yeah, you're probably right about that. But they've probably figured out by now their pards on this side are done for. If we could do some more damage, they might decide to cut their losses and make a run for it."

"Maybe," The Kid said with a shrug. "Or maybe not. Either way, the more of them we can get rid of, the better the odds for us."

"That's what I was thinkin'. I hate to ask it of a fella who's wounded—"

"This?" The Kid gestured toward his bullet-creased arm. "This is nothing to worry about."

Culhane nodded and turned to Lace. "Now, ma'am, as for you—"

"Are you going to start giving me orders now, Ranger Culhane?" she asked. "As much as I've already pitched in to help?"

"Well, now, ma'am, that was what you might call an extreme situation—"

"And it still is," Lace broke in again. "I may not have started out with any personal stake in this, but those outlaws have shot at me, threatened me with death and worse, and killed innocent men."

"They've done even worse than that before you joined up with us, ma'am," Bill Gustaffson said as he helped his brother steady Nick Burton.

"I don't doubt it for a second," Lace said. "So I'm angry, Ranger Culhane, and I intend to do whatever I can to help deal with those villains!"

"I never was much of a hand for arguin' with womenfolks." Culhane sighed. "So I reckon you can come along, but for pete's sake, be careful, will you?"

Lace smiled at him. "I'll try, Ranger," she promised.

The Kid wasn't sure about that. Caution wasn't a natural part of Lace McCall's personality. But he would do what he could to keep her from being too foolhardy.

Anyway, there had been times when her recklessness came in mighty handy.

Culhane turned to Nick. "How about you, son? How are you doin' now?"

Nick looked pale and shaken, but he was standing mostly on his own two feet again. "I . . . I guess I'm okay, Mr. Culhane. My arm hurts where I got shot."

"I expect it does, and it will for a while." Culhane nodded.

"But I can get around all right," Nick went on. "I think I can even ride a horse. If you want me to help you go after the others, I . . . I'll do my best."

Culhane clapped a hand on the shoulder of the young man's unwounded arm. "I know you will. Where's your horse?"

"All of the horses ought to be around here somewhere." The Kid whistled, hoping that would bring the buckskin to him. A moment later, the horse pushed through the brush, followed by the horses belonging to Lace and Nick.

When everyone was mounted, Culhane said, "We'll work our way back to the head of the canyon and cross over to the other side there. Maybe they won't see us comin' and we can get behind the varmints."

"That's what Miss Morrison and I did on this side," The Kid said. "It worked out pretty well."

That was an understatement. They couldn't hope to be that fortunate again.

The riders moved out through the trees. Culhane took the lead, followed by the Gustaffson brothers, then Nick, then Lace and The Kid bringing up the rear.

After they had gone a short distance, Nick dropped back a little so he was riding beside The Kid. "Mr. Morgan . . . can I ask you a question?"

"Sure, Nick," The Kid said.

"When . . . when you shot that outlaw . . . you were aiming at him, right, not me?"

The Kid smiled. "Sure. What reason would I have to try to shoot you?"

"It's just that . . . well, I swear, I *felt* that bullet go right past my ear . . ."

"That's because it did," Lace said. "That's the only way Mr. Morgan could kill that outlaw fast enough to keep him from killing you."

Nick swallowed hard. "Then that was just . . . I don't think anybody's ever made a shot like that before, Mr. Morgan."

"I wouldn't count on that," The Kid said, thinking of some of the stories he had heard about his father. He wouldn't be at all surprised if sometime during The Drifter's long and perilous career as a gunfighter, Frank Morgan had made a shot every bit as amazing . . . or more.

After riding along in silence for a few minutes, Nick said, "I don't remember much for a while after I got shot. One of you patched up my arm for me, right?"

"I did." Lace smiled at him. "I also gave you a couple drinks of whiskey, and you went out like a light."

Nick's earnest young face flushed with embarrassment. "I've never, uh, had much to drink in my life. I guess I'm not used to it."

"That's all right, Nick," The Kid said. "You're young yet. You've got plenty of time."

"I'm not *that* young," Nick said with a scowl as he glanced at Lace. Clearly, he didn't like the idea of her thinking of him as an inexperienced kid.

The ground started to climb under the horses'

hooves. They were getting close to the head of the canyon, The Kid thought.

Culhane turned around in his saddle to ask, "Everybody got plenty of ammunition?"

He got affirmative answers from the other five riders. A minute later, they came up out of the canyon and could see through the low hills back to the west, all the way to the plains where they had ridden for days on the trail of Warren Latch and his gang.

"The ground's pretty rough over there," Culhane said as they reined in. "We may have to dismount and work our way along that ridge on foot."

"That's not a bad idea," The Kid said. "It'll be quieter that way. Latch's men will be less likely to hear us coming."

Thad asked, "You think this man Latch will be with the rest of them? He's the head of the gang, right?"

Culhane said, "That's right, but I've got a hunch he ain't with 'em. I'll bet he left some of his men here to stop us while he and the rest of the gang kept goin'."

"That's the way I see it, too," The Kid said. "We'll catch up to him, but probably not today."

"I don't care how long it takes," Thad said, "as long as he pays for what he and his men did."

"You can count on that, son," Culhane assured him. "Come on."

The canyon was about a quarter mile wide.

They started riding toward the far side, but they had only covered about half that distance when a flicker of movement caught The Kid's eye.

Before he could call out a warning to the others, seven or eight riders came out of the trees up ahead, charging toward them with guns blazing.

CHAPTER 23

The Kid knew instantly what was happening. Members of Latch's gang, the men had realized the guns on the other side of the canyon had gone silent. Figuring out something had happened to the bushwhackers over there, they were coming to find out what that was.

They'd run right into The Kid and his companions, and the battle was joined again.

"Scatter!" Culhane shouted. As close to even as the odds were, staying bunched up was the worst thing they could do, making them easier targets for the outlaws.

It didn't do any good to turn and flee, either. There was no cover close enough for that.

Drawing his Colt, The Kid heeled the buckskin into a run, meeting the outlaws' attack with a charge of his own.

Not surprisingly, Lace did the same thing, veering off to the side to put some distance between her and The Kid at the same time.

Culhane followed their example, angling to The Kid's left while Lace went to the right.

Nick, Thad, and Bill hesitated only for a second. With the other three members of their group showing them what to do, they leaped to the attack as well.

It was a chaotic few moments in the open field at the head of the canyon as guns roared and bullets flew. Swirls of powdersmoke wreathed the galloping figures.

After his first shot, The Kid held his fire until he had a good target. He waited to pull the trigger until the outlaw pounding toward him, shooting wildly, was close. The bullet punched into the man's chest, driving him backward out of the saddle. His left foot got hung up in the stirrup, causing the horse to drag him. More dust rose to mix with the gunsmoke.

The Kid wheeled the buckskin and looked for Lace. He spotted her about twenty yards away, bent far forward over the neck of her mount to make herself a smaller target as she traded shots with one of the desperadoes. She didn't seem aware of the outlaw closing in on her from behind and to the right.

Sending the buckskin lunging in that direction, The Kid snapped a shot at the man but missed. He might not get another chance. The outlaw was drawing a bead on Lace's back.

The Kid did the only thing he could, running the

buckskin right into the outlaw's horse, shoulder to shoulder. The collision sent both horses and both riders tumbling to the ground in a welter of flailing hooves.

Half stunned, The Kid still had the presence of mind to roll away from the confusion. If one of the horses kicked him, it would be the end of the fight for him.

Coughing against the dust clogging his throat, he staggered to his feet with the Colt still in his hand. He looked around for Lace.

Something crashed into him from behind and knocked him down again. His gun went flying as his face plowed into the ground, filling his mouth with dirt and grass. He gagged.

The next instant, an arm snaked around his neck and closed down hard on his throat. With a good grip, the man who had tackled him obviously intended to choke the life out of him.

His eyes full of grit, The Kid blinked furiously in an attempt to clear his sight so he could look for his gun. Half blinded, his blurry gaze fell on the Colt, lying a couple feet in front of him. He reached for it.

At the same moment, the outlaw planted a knee in the middle of The Kid's back and heaved up, tightening the hold on his throat. A red haze settled over his eyes as the air to his lungs was cut off. He felt like everything in his throat was being crushed.

Knowing it would soon be followed by the black of unconsciousness and then death, he got his hands underneath him and levered himself up an inch or so. It gave him enough room to dig his toes into the ground and shove himself forward, a few inches closer to his fallen gun.

The outlaw muttered desperate curses as he continued strangling The Kid.

He must have lost his gun, too, or he wouldn't be trying to choke his enemy to death, the Kid thought, shoving with his feet. He reached for the gun. His fingers came up tantalizingly short of its grips.

He had completely lost track of everything going on around him. All that existed in his world was the ground beneath him, the arm around his neck, and the Colt just out of his reach. As streaks of darkness began to shoot through the red fog surrounding him, he lunged again . . .

And his hand closed on the Colt.

Knowing he had only seconds left before he passed out, The Kid snatched the gun from the ground, shoved the barrel up and back, past his shoulder, and felt it hit something.

He pulled the trigger.

So close to his ear, the report was painfully loud, so loud he was stunned again.

The sudden spray of something hot, wet, and sticky settled against the back of his neck and head. The pressure on his throat was released and his head slumped forward. His cheek rested against the ground as he desperately dragged air into his lungs.

After a moment, the terrible pounding inside The Kid's skull eased, and the frantic feeling that he was about to suffocate slackened as well. A heavy weight still lay on his back. With a groan of effort, he heaved to his side, causing the outlaw to roll away from him. The sight that greeted his still-bleary eyes wasn't a pretty one. He had jammed the Colt's barrel under the outlaw's chin before he pulled the trigger. The shot had blasted away the lower half of the man's face, leaving a gory mess. The blood from the gaping wound had splattered over The Kid's head.

Revulsion roiled his stomach, but he didn't have time to be sick. Still holding the revolver, he staggered to his feet and looked around.

Lace had dismounted, and she ran toward him. "Kid!" she cried. "Oh my God, Kid, you're covered with blood!"

"Not . . . mine," he rasped. Being choked had left him sounding almost as bad as Vint Reilly. He hoped it would go away more quickly than Reilly's condition had.

His right ear was ringing from the proximity of the gunshot. He gave a little shake of his head, hoping that would clear some of the racket.

Lace gripped his arm. "You're not hurt?"

"I'll be fine," he assured her. "Where are . . . the others?"

He looked around. Several other bodies—all members of Latch's gang—were scattered across the open area. Still mounted, Thad and Bill Gustaffson had reached the far side of the clearing. They turned their horses and trotted back toward The Kid and Lace.

"Where are Culhane and Nick?" The Kid asked.

As if in answer to the question, a frantic voice he recognized as Nick Burton's shouted, "Help! We need help over here!"

The Kid and Lace swung around. They saw Nick about thirty yards away, kneeling beside Culhane, who lay on the ground.

Even from that distance, The Kid could see the blood pumping from a wound on the Ranger's leg. He and Lace ran toward Nick and the fallen lawman. The Gustaffsons reached them at the same time.

The Kid quickly asked the brothers, "What about the other outlaws?"

"Only two were left, and they lit out," Bill replied.

"Probably headed back to join up with the rest of their bunch," Thad added.

The Kid thought that was probably right. Throughout the long chase, Latch's men had turned and run every time the odds went against them.

Lace pushed Nick aside none too gently and examined the wound on Culhane's leg. The unconscious Ranger's face was gray. He had already lost a lot of blood. If they didn't get the bleeding stopped soon, Culhane would die.

As Lace ripped the leg of Culhane's bullet-torn jeans even more, she told The Kid, "Get his belt and gun."

He knew what she meant to do and agreed with her. Unbuckling Culhane's belt and pulling it free, The Kid handed it to Lace. He picked up the gun the Ranger had dropped, then lifted Culhane's leg so she could wrap the belt around it.

She made a loop with the belt, and The Kid thrust the barrel of Culhane's gun into it and began to turn the weapon, tightening the belt into a makeshift tourniquet. As he increased the pressure, the flow of blood from the bullet hole slowed dramatically.

"Somebody give me some cloth from your shirt," Lace ordered.

Thad and Bill ripped pieces from their shirts and offered them to her. She took the one Bill held out and wadded it up, then pressed it hard against the wound.

She held it there like that for several minutes while The Kid hung on to the gun and maintained the tightness of the tourniquet. When Lace took the cloth away from the bullet hole, The Kid saw that the bleeding had just about stopped. Very little blood oozed from the wound.

"Nick, there's a flask in my saddlebags," Lace said. "Go get it." With a grim smile, she added, "Just don't drink any of the whiskey in it. We can't afford to have you going to sleep again."

"Awww . . ."

"Go!"

He went, breaking into a run toward Lace's saddle mount.

The Kid said, "Thad, Bill, keep a close watch to make sure none of Latch's men come back and take us by surprise."

"Sure, Mr. Morgan," Thad said. "I don't think they will, though, the way they were running when they left here."

Nick came back with the flask. Lace took the other piece of cloth and soaked it with whiskey, then used it to swab away some of the blood and clean the wound. She dribbled some of the fiery liquor directly into the bullet hole.

"We can't keep this tourniquet on too long," The Kid warned. "If we do, he's liable to lose that leg."

"It hasn't been too long yet," Lace said. "Trust me, Kid, I've dealt with this kind of wound before."

Thad asked, "Why does she keep calling you Kid, Mr. Morgan? Something about that sounds a mite familiar."

"Son of a gun!" Bill suddenly exclaimed. "He's Kid Morgan, the gunfighter! I've read about him!"

Lace glanced at The Kid and smiled. "Looks like your secret's out."

"It was never that much of a secret." The Kid shrugged.

"Well, I'm glad I don't have to keep it anymore," Nick said.

The Gustaffson brothers looked at him. Bill said, "You knew about this?"

"Yeah," Nick replied, looking a little ashamed. "I'm sorry, fellas. Mr. Morgan asked me to keep quiet about it, and I promised him I would."

"Then how did Miss Morrison know?"

"Because she's not Miss Morrison," The Kid said. No point in *any* of them keeping secrets any longer. As badly wounded as Culhane was, he wasn't going to be in command of the posse anymore. "Her name's Lace McCall. She's a bounty hunter."

Thad let out a surprised whistle. "I didn't know there were any lady bounty hunters."

"I expect there's plenty in this world you don't know," Lace said. "No offense. Kid, let off some on that belt."

The Kid eased the pressure while Lace bent forward and studied the wound. It began to bleed again, but not nearly as fast as it had been before.

"I think we can handle that," she said. "I'll tie a

bandage on it. He's going to need some actual medical attention, though."

"Culhane told me there wasn't a doctor back in Stubbtown," The Kid said. "We'll have to keep going until we find a settlement where there's a sawbones."

"What about Latch and the rest of his gang?" Bill asked. "Are we still going after them?"

With a grim look on his face, The Kid replied, "I reckon that'll depend on what we find when we get down there in that canyon."

CHAPTER 24

Lace had done a makeshift but thorough job of bandaging Culhane's wounded leg and bound it up tightly. It appeared the risk of the Ranger bleeding to death was over.

But he was still in bad shape. Culhane hadn't had a chance to tell the other members of the posse that The Kid was going to take over if he was incapacitated. The Kid couldn't help wondering how the others were going to take it.

Some of them wouldn't take it well, he thought.

It was too soon to worry about that, however. The first thing was to find all the men who had survived the ambush and get them together again.

Regaining consciousness, Culhane groaned and leaned on the saddle horn as Thad and Bill steadied him on his horse. "Wha . . . what happened?" he managed to ask.

"You were shot in the leg, Ranger," The Kid told him. "We came close to losing you, but I think you'll be all right. Can you stay in the saddle, or do we need to tie you onto your horse?"

Culhane grimaced. "The day I . . . can't ride . . . you might as well go ahead . . . and put me in the ground!"

He looked around, but The Kid couldn't tell how much he was actually seeing.

"What about . . . those owlhoots?" Culhane went on.

"We killed some of them, and the others ran off. We haven't seen hide nor hair of them since, and all the shooting has stopped."

"They gave up and . . . went back to Latch."

The Kid nodded. "That's what we figured, too."

"Did we . . . lose anybody else . . . in this fight?"

"No, you were the only one who was hit."

"Well, that's . . . lucky, anyway."

Thad said, "Ranger, did you know Mr. Morgan is really Kid Morgan, the famous gunfighter?"

"And that Miss Morrison's really a bounty hunter who's after Latch, too?" Bill added.

"We can go into all that later," The Kid said. "Right now we need to find the rest of our bunch."

Culhane eyed him speculatively. "I knew there was somethin' . . . different about you, mister," he muttered. "You ain't . . . wanted by the law, are you?"

"If I was, she'd already have me hog-tied so she could collect the reward on me," The Kid told him with a nod toward Lace.

She laughed. "He's right about that, Mr. Culhane. My name is really Lace McCall, by the way."

"Pleased to meet you . . . again, ma'am," Culhane said.

The others mounted up, and the group moved out, taking it slow because of Culhane. The Kid and Lace took the lead with the Kid's pack horse following them. The Gustaffsons and Nick rode bunched up around Culhane so they could reach him easily and brace him up if he started to fall.

The Kid and Lace rode with fully loaded Winchesters across the saddles in front of them as they descended into the canyon. Their eyes never stopped moving as their gazes roamed across the canyon and up the slopes on the sides.

After narrowly surviving one trap, they didn't want to ride right into another one.

Staying in the open, they hoped to attract the attention of the surviving posse members. A few minutes later, several men on horseback emerged from some trees and rode quickly toward them.

The Kid recognized Ed Marchman in the lead. The stocky storekeeper's two employees, Clyde Fenner and Jack Hogan, were with him, as usual, along with a couple of other men from Fire Hill.

"Are the outlaws gone?" Marchman asked as he rode up and reined in.

"They seem to be," The Kid replied. "Most of the ones who bushwhacked us are dead."

"What happened to Ranger Culhane?" Clyde said. "Did he get shot?"

"That's right. It's a serious wound, but we hope he'll be all right."

Culhane lifted his head. His face was pale and haggard, but he looked determined to say something. "Marchman," he got out. "You listen . . . to me."

Marchman brought his horse closer. "Sure, Ranger. What is it?"

"I'm in no shape . . . to be in charge of this posse—"

"And you want me to take over?" Marchman interrupted. "I suppose I could—"

"No . . . blast it!" Culhane broke in. "I was about to say . . . Morgan's runnin' things now. He's . . . in command."

Marchman's eyes widened in surprise. "Morgan!" he exclaimed. "But he's not even from Fire Hill!"

"Don't matter. He's . . . the best man for the job."

Marchman's features hardened into a glare. "He's not a lawman. We don't have to take orders from him."

"But I'm still . . . a Texas Ranger," Culhane said. "And I'm tellin' you . . . Morgan's in charge."

Marchman turned angrily toward The Kid. "You put him up to this, and he's hurt too bad to fight you on it," he accused.

The Kid fixed Marchman with a cold stare. "This is all Culhane's idea. I didn't ask for the job. You can believe that or not. I don't give a damn either way. But he's asked for my help, and I told him I'd do it. So that's the way it's going to be."

"Maybe. Maybe not," Marchman snapped.

The men from Fire Hill moved up closer as if in support of him.

Lace's voice cut sharply through the tension. "What are you going to do, start shooting at each other now?" she demanded. "Have you all gone loco?"

"This is none of your business, Miss Morrison," Marchman said coldly.

"You're wrong about that, Mr. Marchman," Thad said. "She's really a bounty hunter, and she's after Latch just like we are."

Clyde said, "I'm gettin' confused—"

"Shut up!" Marchman said. "I suppose we can hash all this out later. Right now we need to see if we can find the rest of our men . . . and bury our dead, if need be."

There would be a need for that, The Kid thought. He was certain of it.

218

They spent the rest of the afternoon scouring the canyon for survivors and burying the three men who had been fatally wounded in the ambush. Two of the men were from Fire Hill, and the third was an M-B Connected puncher. Four men besides The Kid and Nick had suffered minor wounds. Of the survivors, Culhane was the most badly wounded.

The hills, ridges, and canyons of the rugged country continued as far as the eye could see. Compared to the more arid terrain farther west, a number of creeks ran through it so there was plenty of water for the men and horses. The posse made camp on a broad stretch of level ground next to one of those cold, fast-flowing streams.

Despite the fact that they hadn't caught even a glimpse of Latch's men since the outlaws had abandoned the ambush and fled, The Kid expected trouble. As darkness crept across the Texas sky and the stars began to come out, he got it.

Ed Marchman stalked to the center of the camp and stood next to the fire that had been built. He planted his fists on his hips and said in a loud voice, "Everybody listen to me!"

The Kid and Lace had made Culhane comfortable on some blankets spread over thick grass. The Ranger had a rolled-up blanket tucked under his head as a pillow, and he was either asleep or unconscious. In his weakened condition, the ride down the canyon had worn him out.

The Kid rose from where he'd been kneeling beside Culhane and faced Marchman. "What is it you intend to do?"

"I'm going to tell the rest of these men exactly what's going on," Marchman snapped. "They have a right to know, and a right to make up their own minds about what we do next."

"You know that's not what Ranger Culhane wanted." Lace stepped forward into the firelight. Her auburn hair was loose, hanging around her shoulders, and the light from the flames made it look even more red.

"Culhane's badly injured," Marchman said. "He's not running things around here anymore. That's what we have to decide now."

Abel Gustaffson said, "What are you talking about?"

Marchman leveled a finger at The Kid. "He thinks *he's* in charge now."

"That's what Ranger Culhane wanted," Nick said. "We all heard him say so."

"We're not Texas Rangers. He's not in charge of us, and we can do what we think is best."

Some of the men looked dubious about that. Everybody in Texas knew the power of the Rangers, and they didn't want to go against the wishes of anybody who wore the famous star-in-a-circle badge.

"Get on with what you want to say, Marchman."

220

The Kid was tired, and he didn't have any patience for nonsense.

"I'm saying that somebody else should be in charge of this posse, somebody who has a personal stake in bringing Latch and his men to justice. Not some gunfighter who's probably a bounty hunter just like this redheaded woman!"

"You make that sound like you're calling me an impolite name, mister," Lace said in a quiet, dangerous tone.

Marchman shook his head. "Sorry," he muttered. "But we've all heard the talk. You're after the rewards for Latch and his men, and Morgan's a well-known killer, the next thing to an outlaw himself. The rest of us are out for justice, not blood money!"

"Justice . . . or revenge?" The Kid asked.

"It's the same . . . thing." Vint Reilly stepped forward. It hurt just listening to how he had to force the words from his damaged throat.

"Vint's right," Abel Gustaffson added. "If we're having a vote, I think he should be the one to lead this posse since Culhane can't anymore."

Marchman looked surprised. "Wait a minute—"

"You thought you'd . . . just appoint yourself . . . as leader?" Reilly asked. "You lost . . . a building . . . some merchandise . . . some of us here . . . lost a lot more than that."

"Now, Vint, I know that," Marchman said. "And I'm not trying to stir up trouble."

That was exactly what he was trying to do, The Kid thought. Marchman had chafed under Culhane's command right from the start, and now he wanted to wield some power himself.

"I'm not sure why we're even talking about this," The Kid said. "We all want the same thing. We want Latch and his men either dead or behind bars."

"Marchman's right . . . about one thing," Reilly said. "You don't have . . . a stake in this, Morgan. When there's a decision . . . to be made . . . you might pull back instead of . . . going all out."

"I won't risk anybody's life needlessly, if that's what you mean."

"Let's put it to a vote," Gustaffson urged. "I say we put Vint Reilly in charge of this posse."

Marchman looked flustered. "But Vint's hurt, too. He's badly burned, so badly he's been nipping at that bottle of painkiller ever since we left Fire Hill!"

"His mind seems clear to me," Gustaffson said. "He knows what's got to be done. And from what I've heard, he's kept up with everybody, right from the start."

Thad put a hand on his father's arm. "Pa, I'm not so sure—"

Gustaffson jerked his arm away. "I'm your father! Are you gonna argue with me, boy?"

Thad glanced at Bill and then shook his head. "No, sir, I reckon I'm not."

"Neither am I," Bill put in. "But that doesn't mean you're right, Pa."

"You'll do as I say, that's all I care about," Gustaffson snapped. He looked at the others. "How about it? Put it to a vote?" Gustaffson flung a hand toward Reilly. "Are you going to vote against a man who's lost as much as Vint has?"

Nick said, "I think we should do what Ranger Culhane wanted and put Mr. Morgan in charge. He's done more to bust up Latch's gang than any of the rest of us. Him and Miss McCall, anyway. That's the way the M-B Connected is voting."

He turned to look at the group of punchers who rode for his grandfather, and despite his small size, he seemed a lot bigger right then. One by one, the cowboys nodded their agreement.

"What about . . . the rest of us?" Reilly demanded of the men from Fire Hill.

Marchman still looked torn. He had wanted the power for himself, but at the same time, he didn't want The Kid taking control of the posse.

The Kid could tell that was what was going through the man's mind.

Grudgingly, Marchman said, "I can go along with putting Vint in charge. I've known him for a long time. He's a good man."

Not surprisingly, Fenner and Hogan spoke up, agreeing with their boss. That was all it took to break the logjam. The other men from Fire Hill went along with naming Reilly as the new leader

223

of the posse. The vote of Abel Gustaffson and the reluctant votes of his sons gave Reilly the victory.

"When Culhane wakes up, this little election of yours won't mean a damned thing," Lace said hotly. "So you'd better enjoy it while you can."

"Take it easy," The Kid told her. "It's not important. We're going after Latch either way."

"Yes, but—" She stopped and blew out an exasperated breath. "Fine. But I'm still going after that bounty."

"I don't think anybody here is fool enough to try to stop you," The Kid said with a smile.

CHAPTER 25

The posse was divided after that, the men from the M-B Connected gathering on one side of the fire while the others clustered around Vint Reilly and asked him what his plans were.

"We'll push on . . . as fast and hard as we can," Reilly said. "We've only got . . . a couple more days to catch Latch and what's left of . . . his gang."

The Kid agreed with that. Time was running out on them. But for tonight, anyway, there was nothing more they could do.

The blood that had splattered on his head had dried to a sticky mess in his hair, so he got a clean shirt from his saddlebags and told Lace, "I'm going upstream to see if I can find a little pool or something where I can clean up. Can you stay here and keep an eye on Culhane?"

"Of course. You go ahead, Kid."

He followed the stream around a couple bends and then heard a noise he recognized as that of a waterfall. A moment later he came upon the place.

The creek flowed over a bluff and fell straight down for about twenty feet into a pool at the base of the bluff. In the moonlight, he could see it was big enough to bathe in. He hoped it was deep enough.

He stripped off his bloodstained shirt first and washed it out as best he could. The water was chilly, telling him it came from springs deep in the earth. When he thought he had gotten most of the blood out of the fabric, he spread the shirt on a rock to dry.

The Kid took off his boots and socks, followed by his trousers. He waded into the pool clad only in the bottom half of a pair of long underwear.

The water was cold enough to take his breath away when he plunged his whole body into it. Coming up for air, he took a deep breath and dived underwater again, keeping his head under the surface as he scrubbed at the blood on his skin and in his hair.

Raising up a few moments later, he was surprised to see someone standing on the bank at the edge of the pool. For a split second he wished he hadn't left his gunbelt coiled on the same rock as his trousers, but then he recognized Lace.

"Sorry if I startled you, Kid. I would have called out, but I saw that you were under the water, and didn't know if you could hear me."

"What are you doing here? You're supposed to be watching Culhane."

"Culhane's asleep. He's not going anywhere, and nobody's going to hurt him." She started to unbutton her shirt. "Besides, you're not the only one who's gotten grubby enough to need a bath."

The Kid didn't believe for a second that a bath was the only reason Lace was there.

"Aren't you going to ask me to turn around?" he said as she took off her shirt and reached for the waist of the riding skirt.

"Well, now, there wouldn't be a lot of point in that, would there?" She pushed the skirt down over her hips and stepped out of it, leaving her wearing only a thin shift and her boots. "I mean, after all we've been through together . . ."

"Then I won't turn around or close my eyes."

"Fine by me." Sitting down on one of the rocks, she took off her boots. "How's the water?"

"Cold."

"That's all right. It was a hot day. I could use something to cool me down."

"This ought to do it," The Kid said.

"That's what I'm hoping." She stepped into the pool.

He noticed she shivered a little from the temperature of the water as she walked toward him. He ducked his head under the surface and continued washing his thick, fair hair in an attempt to get all the blood out of it.

When he came up, he didn't see Lace. He knew she hadn't left, so he wasn't surprised when she broke the surface a few feet from him. Her red hair was dark in the moonlight as water plastered it to her head.

"Let me help you," she said. "Turn around."

The Kid did as she told him, but not before he noticed how the wet shift clung to her body. Her nipples, hardened by the cold water and perhaps by something else, stood out plainly against the thin fabric.

She moved up behind him and started rubbing her hands over his shoulders and through his hair. "You looked pretty gruesome earlier," she said quietly. "All that blood on you like that."

"I'm just glad it wasn't mine."

"I am, too." She continued washing his hair but paused in her speaking before she went on. "I should have stayed in touch and told you I was out hunting bounty again, Kid."

"It takes two people to stay in touch. I didn't do any better job of it than you did."

"I really appreciate everything you've done for me . . . and for my family."

"Thank Conrad Browning the next time you

see him, whenever that is," The Kid said gruffly.

"I would, if I thought I was ever going to run into him again. But the only one I see is this stubborn Kid Morgan."

The Kid didn't say anything to that. He wasn't going to get into a debate with her over whether or not he should resume his life as Conrad Browning. He had made up his mind on the matter, and that was that.

After a moment, Lace went on. "Anyway, I'm sorry I didn't write more often and let you know how we were doing. I can't believe it was just blind luck that brought us together again."

"What else would you call it?"

"Oh, I don't know . . . Fate? Destiny?"

"I'm not sure I believe in those things any-more."

"You don't believe the world ever makes sense? You think things just happen without any real reason for them?"

The Kid took a step away and turned to face her. "What kind of reason could there be for Warren Latch to burn a whole town to the ground and kill so many people there? How could there be any plan behind them murdering Abel Gustaffson's wife and daughters?" He shook his head. "You can't tell me that makes any sense. It's just evil. You can't explain it, you can't predict it, and most of the time you can't stop it."

"Is that any reason not to try?"

He smiled in the moonlight. "I never said that. Maybe we can't win in the end . . . but we can always try."

She looked at him silently for a moment. "You know, my hair could use washing, too."

"Go ahead. Nobody's stopping you."

She made a fist and punched him lightly on his bare chest. "So it's all right for me to wash your hair, but you won't return the favor?"

"I didn't say that, either." He moved closer to her again and lifted his hands to run his fingers through the wet strands of her hair. He started massaging her scalp.

She closed her eyes and tilted her head back a little as she made a small sound of pleasure in her throat. The gap between them shrank until their bodies were pressed against each other.

The Kid could feel every contour of her shape through the thin shift. He moved his hands to the back of her head and cupped it as he brought his mouth down on hers. As soon as he'd seen Lace standing at the edge of the pool, he had known it was what she intended to happen.

Other women had offered themselves to him in the past, after Rebel was murdered. He had turned down all of them . . . except Lace. There was something different about her, something that drew him.

He would never stop grieving for his lost love, for the woman who, along with Frank Morgan, had totally transformed his life from what it had been before he met them.

But time had moved on and so had he. The human need for closeness was still inside him, as it was in Lace. They reached out to each other, seeking to discover if it was the right time and place . . .

There was no doubt about the answer.

Slim Duval and Mitch Holton picked up three more men from the gang as they fled the canyon where the trap that was supposed to wipe out the posse had gone so terribly, horribly wrong.

Five men out of twenty-two were all that remained from the group Warren Latch had left behind. What had started out as an unstoppable force of forty men had dwindled to a little more than half of their original number.

It was possible that damned posse outnumbered them now, Duval thought bitterly as he and his companions rode through the night.

"You think we're gonna be able to find the rendezvous in the dark?" Holton asked, breaking into Duval's sour reverie.

"What? Of course we can find it. I know this country." Duval hoped his resentful certainty was correct. The way things had been going recently, he wasn't sure about anything anymore.

The raid had started out profitable and gone so well, right up until the time they had ridden out of Fire Hill, leaving the settlement in flames behind them. It was almost like they had been cursed ever since.

Duval was too much of a hardheaded realist to believe in curses, but that was what it seemed like. The posse had dogged the gang's trail with more stubborn persistence than he had seen in any other posse. And every time Latch's men tried to do something about it, they wound up suffering more losses than they inflicted.

"No need to bite my head off," Holton said in a surly tone. "You can't blame a fella for bein' worried, the way things have been goin', Slim."

That was exactly what Duval had just been thinking. So the gang's bad luck was on the minds of the other men, too. How could it not be? Almost half of the men who'd set out from San Antonio would never be coming back.

He forced a smile onto his face. "Sorry, Mitch. Reckon my nerves are worn a little thin."

"Mine would be, too," one of the other men put in, "if I had to go back to Warren Latch and tell him that I failed to stop that posse . . . again."

Duval almost pulled his gun, twisted around in the saddle, and shot the mouthy son of a bitch. With an effort, he controlled the impulse. The gang had lost enough men already without them starting to kill each other.

"If you want to be in charge next time, Jenkins,

I'll talk to Warren and see if I can convince him to go along with that."

"What?" The man sounded surprised. "Hell, no! I never said I wanted to be in charge of anything, Slim. I'm sorry if that's what it sounded like."

"That's what it sounded like, all right," Duval snapped. "Maybe you'd better start paying more attention to what comes out of that piehole of yours."

"Yeah, yeah, sure," Jenkins muttered. "Sorry."

"I'm not sure the boss will try to stop that posse anymore," Holton said. "Maybe it would be best if we just cut and run and try to beat them back to San Antone."

That would have been the smartest course of action all along, Duval reflected.

Latch took the posse's stubbornness as a personal insult. The way he saw it, the pursuers from Fire Hill were violating the natural order of things, which was that Warren Latch ought to be able to do whatever he damned well pleased and get away with it.

They ought to be getting close to the rendezvous, Duval thought as he scanned the horizon. Sure enough, the moon provided enough light for him to spot a pair of hills crowded so close together they looked like the humps on a camel's back in a picture he had seen in a book one time.

People called that landmark Camelback Hill, even though there were actually two hills. At the base of it was a hollow where Latch and the rest of the gang would be camped.

Duval pointed out the landmark to his companions, and a short time later they rode up to the camp, where a large fire was burning. Latch strode forward to meet them, followed by several others.

"Slim?" Latch said in a questioning tone. "I only see . . . five of you." Latch's voice hardened. "Where are the others?"

Duval didn't answer immediately. In the process of dismounting, he finished swinging down from his horse before he sighed. "We lost them, Warren."

"Lost them?" Latch repeated. "What do you mean, lost them? Did you get separated—"

"They're dead, all right?" Duval broke in, knowing it was a mistake to speak that way to Latch, but too tired and dispirited to control his own anger. "That damned posse broke out of our trap and killed the rest of them!"

Latch stared at him, obviously thunderstruck by the news. In the flickering light from the fire, the outlaw leader's lean face slowly darkened with fury. "You let them escape . . . *again?*" Latch's voice trembled. "You had the high ground, you had cover, all you had to do was shoot them!"

"We got some of them," Duval protested. "But the rest of the bunch scattered too fast for us to do much damage, and then somehow"—he'd been struggling to figure it out, but couldn't—"some of them got behind our men on the north slope and started a rock slide that wiped them out."

"You're sure about that?"

"I didn't see the bodies, but I saw the slide and heard them screaming, and then all the shooting stopped over there. What else was I supposed to think?" Duval scrubbed a hand wearily over his face before he went on. "I took some of the men and we tried to circle around there and find out what happened. We ran right into a bunch of those bastards. We hit 'em hard, but they hit us harder. All we could do, the few of us who were left, was get out of there while we were still alive."

Latch's right hand came up suddenly, and one of those fancy, foreign-made pistols was in it. Duval found himself staring down the Mauser's barrel. He knew if Latch pulled the trigger, his head would be blown away in a matter of seconds. He'd never been closer to death than he was at that instant.

"I ought to kill you," Latch said into the tense silence hanging over the camp. Nobody was going to come to Duval's aid or defense. Latch went on. "I've sent you after this posse three times, and each time you've come back with fewer men. No one fails me that many times, Slim."

Duval's pride made him defend himself. "I've done the best I could, Warren. The cards have been against me."

"This isn't a game." Latch pointed the Mauser at the sky, took a deep breath, and holstered the pistol. "But we've been together for too long, you and I, and I need every man I've got in case that posse catches up to us before we reach San Antonio."

Duval managed not to heave a sigh of relief that Latch had spared his life. "Maybe we ought to push on tonight. There's enough light we shouldn't get off the trail."

Latch appeared to consider the suggestion for a moment, but then he shook his head. "No, the men and the horses all need rest. We'll make better time tomorrow if we stay here tonight."

Duval nodded. "Whatever you say, Warren."

"What I say is those men deserve to suffer for being so foolhardy as to pursue us like this," Latch declared. "That's what I say."

Duval didn't like the sound of that. When Latch's pride was wounded, the man was capable of doing almost anything.

But not even Warren Latch would do something so loco as turning back and trying to hit that posse *again,* especially after everything that had happened so far.

Would he?

CHAPTER 26

When The Kid and Lace got back to the camp, they went straight to the place where Asa Culhane lay on the blankets.

His head hanging forward on his chest, Nick sat beside the wounded Ranger, dozing. He jerked awake as The Kid knelt beside him and lightly touched his shoulder.

"Oh! Mr. Morgan . . . Sorry I jumped like that."

"I'm sorry I startled you, Nick," The Kid said. "How's Culhane doing?"

"He's just been sleeping. I guess he's all right."

The Kid looked around the camp. Some of the men from Fire Hill were sleeping, but the rest were still huddled together on the far side of the campfire, talking quietly among themselves. Abel Gustaffson was with them, too, sitting beside Vint Reilly.

"Any other trouble?" The Kid asked.

Nick shook his head. "No, they've just been sitting over there talking. I don't know what it's about. We all want the same thing. It looks like we ought to be able to work together."

"You'd think so," Lace put in. "Why don't you get some sleep, Nick? I'll keep an eye on Ranger Culhane."

"Are you sure, ma'am?"

"I'm certain. And while you're at it, why don't you stop calling me ma'am? I'm not really all that much older than you, you know. Old enough to be your big sister, maybe, but definitely not your mother."

"Yes'm, I know that . . . I mean, Miss McCall . . ."

"Just make it Lace," she suggested.

"All right . . . Lace," Nick swallowed. "That sure is a pretty name."

"Thank you." She pointed to the bedrolls spread near the fire. "Now go and sleep."

"All right."

Nick went and stretched out while The Kid and Lace sat beside Culhane. The youngster turned his back to them, and a few minutes later they heard the deep, regular sound of his breathing as he slept.

"That boy's in love with you," The Kid said quietly to Lace.

"What? You're loco!"

"Maybe, but not about that," The Kid insisted. "And you ought to be able to see it. I'm sure Nick's not the first young man to succumb to your charms."

"He's not even the only one in this posse," she said with a soft laugh.

The Kid rather would have dwelled on sweet memories of what had happened earlier in the evening, but something was nagging at him.

"I need to go talk to Reilly." He got to his feet.

A frown replaced Lace's smile. "I'm not sure you're going to be welcome over on that side of the fire."

"They'll talk to me." His flinty tone of voice left no doubt about that.

He walked around the fire. Reilly, Gustaffson, and the others fell silent when they saw him coming.

"What do you want, Morgan?" Marchman asked. Since his own bid for power had failed, it looked like he intended to make himself a confidante of Reilly and Gustaffson by sucking up to them.

"Just checking to make sure you've posted guards," The Kid said.

"My boys are out there standing watch," Gustaffson said. "So are a couple others."

"Good. It's not likely Latch will make another move against us so soon, but we can't be sure about that."

"Let him," Reilly said. "If he comes after us, that saves us the trouble . . . of going after him."

"We don't want to ride into any more traps," The Kid warned. "That last one could have been the end of us."

And it likely would have, he thought, if not for what he and Lace had done. He wasn't sure any of these men really understood what a close call it had been.

"All I care about . . . is killing as many of those outlaws . . . as I can," Reilly said. "I don't care . . . how we do it."

"I do," The Kid snapped. "I don't want any more of us to die unnecessarily."

"Dying to settle a score like all of us have might be necessary," Gustaffson said. "We don't need you to tell us what to do, Morgan."

"That's right," Marchman added. "If you don't like it, you can saddle your horse and ride out."

Under different circumstances, The Kid might have done just that. He didn't have a personal grudge against Warren Latch . . . or at least he hadn't until Latch's men had tried several times to kill him. Nor was he a sworn lawman like Culhane. He didn't have anything holding him there.

Except for Lace, he thought as he glanced across the campfire at her. If he believed she would come with him, they could both leave.

But that wasn't going to happen. She wanted that bounty, and wouldn't give it up. Even if he rode away, she would stick with the posse.

Then there was Culhane, who had been friendly to him, and Nick Burton, who looked up to him, and the other men from the M-B Connected who were there only because they rode for the brand and their boss had sent them after Latch. The Kid didn't want to abandon any of them, either.

"I'll stick," he said.

Reilly shrugged. "Suit . . . yourself." He took a little nip from the brown bottle.

The Kid could have been mistaken, but he thought he caught a faint scent of putrefying flesh mixed in with the smoke from the fire. It probably came from under those bandages.

Reilly's untreated burns were doing more than keeping him in unending agony. There was a good chance they were rotting his flesh away, a rot that would penetrate deeper and deeper until it consumed him.

He seemed to know he was doomed, and didn't mind taking other men to hell with him if it meant he would get what he wanted before he died.

That one goal was Warren Latch's destruction. Not an unworthy ambition . . .

But how many lives was it going to cost?

Reilly, Gustaffson, and Marchman had everyone up early the next morning. That was nothing unusual. Culhane had done the same thing, pushing the men of the posse at a pace as hard as he thought they could stand.

Culhane was awake and able to drink a little coffee, although he refused to eat anything.

"Y'all better just go ahead and leave me right here," he urged The Kid and Lace. "I'll rest up for a few days, and then I'll be ready to ride again."

"You're in no shape to be left alone," Lace said.

"I'm in no shape to ride, either," Culhane told her with a bleak smile.

"He's right. If he stays in the saddle all day today, that wound is probably going to break open and start bleeding again. I'm not sure he can spare any more blood." The Kid looked at Lace, rubbing his chin as he frowned in thought. "What we need is a wagon."

Understanding dawned in Lace's green eyes. "That's right. If we had a wagon, we could make Mr. Culhane comfortable in it and get him to a settlement where there's a doctor without risking him bleeding to death."

The Kid nodded. "There's bound to be a ranch or a farm somewhere around here where we can borrow a wagon or a buckboard."

"I'm layin' right here while you're debatin' my future, you know," Culhane pointed out. "And you ain't got time to go huntin' up a wagon so you can haul me around. You got a bunch of no-good outlaws to catch, remember?"

"We're not likely to forget that," Lace told him. "But we're not going to leave you here to die, either."

Gustaffson stomped around from the other side of the fire. "You're supposed to be getting ready to ride. What's the holdup over here?"

"The Ranger's in no shape to ride," The Kid said. "We're going to have to get a wagon for him."

Gustaffson snorted. "Well, if you can snap your fingers and make one appear, Morgan, you go right ahead. But make it fast, because we're pulling out soon."

Despite what The Kid had said the night before, Culhane's condition had made him change his mind. "No. I'm going to look for a ranch where I can borrow a wagon. Lace is going to stay here and take care of Culhane while I'm gone. Once we've tended to that, we'll catch up to you."

"Wait just a minute," Lace said sharply. "I don't recall telling you that you can make decisions for me, Kid."

"Then you go find the wagon and I'll stay here."

Culhane said, "You two stop squabblin' and listen to me. I'll be all right here by myself for a while. Prop me up against a tree, leave me a canteen and a little food, and make sure my rifle and revolver are in reach in case any wild critters come along, and I won't need nobody watchin' over me."

Lace dropped to a knee beside him. "Are you sure about that, Mr. Culhane?"

"Yes, ma'am, I am," he declared. "I won't go to movin' around and bust that bullet hole open again. You got my word on that."

Lace looked up at The Kid. "In that case, I'm going with the posse. You can find the wagon, Kid."

He frowned at her. "Are you sure about that?"

"Just as sure as Mr. Culhane is that he'll be all right."

The Kid saw that it wasn't going to do a bit of good to argue with her. The lure of the ten-thousand-dollar reward for Warren Latch, plus the bounties on the heads of the other outlaws, was too much for Lace to resist.

For a second he considered offering to make up the lost bounties from Conrad Browning's riches. He could even double them and never miss the money. But if he did that, she was liable to spit in his face, and he knew it. Lace McCall's pride was a powerful thing.

"All right. But be careful."

She flashed him a grin. "Aren't I always?"

No, he thought, she wasn't.

And that was the problem. She was going to be part of a posse led by a man who had quite possibly been driven mad by grief and pain, followed by a lot of other men who were also consumed with the need for vengeance.

Time was running out on them. That could cause even sane, level-headed men to do foolish things. In the case of Vint Reilly, Abel Gustaffson, and Ed Marchman . . . well, there was just no telling what they might do. No telling at all.

"I'll catch up as soon as I can," The Kid promised.

He worried that might not be soon enough.

Chapter 27

Where there were cows, there were people who owned those cows was a good rule of thumb.

So when The Kid came across cattle grazing in a small valley densely carpeted with grass, he knew he was close to a ranch.

He had ridden northeast when he left the posse, toward a settlement called Bandera. Culhane had told him it was large enough that several doctors could probably be found there.

If it turned out to be necessary, The Kid would ride all the way there, find one of the doctors, and take him back to Culhane, at gunpoint if he had to.

However, he didn't want to do that. It would take longer and delay him in rejoining the posse. His hope was to find someone willing to fetch Culhane and take him to the settlement.

The Kid rode closer to the cattle and checked the brand burned into the hide of a rangy old steer. It was an arrowhead shape with the number seven inside it. The Arrowhead 7, he supposed the ranch was called.

He was wondering how to go about finding the ranch headquarters when a rifle cracked somewhere not far off. The bullet didn't come close enough for him to hear it, but he had a hunch it was a warning shot directed at him.

The sound of hoofbeats from his right made him turn in that direction. A couple riders were coming fast toward him.

He left his Winchester in the saddle boot and kept his hand well away from his Colt as the men approached. That was taking a chance, but they had fired only one shot. He didn't think they wanted to kill him.

As they rode up to him, the men split up so they could cover him better. They were relatively young, but didn't look like greenhorns.

Taking note of their coppery skin and high-cheekboned faces, The Kid realized with a certain amount of surprise that they were Indians. They wore typical range clothes any white or black cowboy might wear.

"Mister, if you're thinkin' about rustlin' that stock, you can just forget about it," one of the men said as they reined in. He had a rifle out, and The Kid figured he was the one who had fired the shot. The other man had a rifle with him, but it was still resting snugly in the saddle boot.

"Rustling was the farthest thing from my mind," The Kid said. "I'm not looking for trouble. I need help. A friend of mine is wounded a few miles from here. I'm looking for a wagon and some-body to take him to a doctor."

"That's an interestin' story, but how do we know it's true?"

"I can't prove it," The Kid admitted. "But my

friend's a Texas Ranger. He gave me this to show to anybody I came across if they needed convincing." He reached into his shirt pocket, aware the two men were watching him closely, and took out Culhane's badge. He extended his hand with the silver star in a silver circle lying on his palm.

"That's a Ranger badge, all right, Tom," said the man who hadn't pulled his rifle.

"Yeah, and where'd he get it?" Tom snapped. "He could've killed the Ranger and taken it off his body."

The Kid shook his head. "I give you my word I'm telling the truth."

Tom regarded The Kid suspiciously. After a moment, he said, "Chuck, you ride back and tell Pa what's going on. I'll go with this man and see about this so-called friend of his."

"I don't know if that's a good idea—"

"Yeah, well, you're not the ramrod of this outfit, are you?" Tom snapped. "Do what I told you."

"Bring a wagon back with you," The Kid suggested. "You'll need it for Ranger Culhane."

"Tom?" Chuck asked.

After a moment, Tom nodded. "Yeah, bring the wagon, just in case he's tellin' the truth. Where exactly is it we're headed?"

The Kid had been keeping track of landmarks as he rode. He turned in the saddle and pointed. "Past a hogback ridge, between a couple flat-topped hills, through a valley, and along a creek for about half a mile or so," he explained.

"That's not a creek," Tom said. "That's the Medina River."

"All right, then. Right there on the Medina River where it makes a bend between a pair of bluffs."

"I can find the place," Chuck said confidently. "You're sure you want me to go, Tom?"

"Get a move on," Tom ordered.

Chuck wheeled his horse and rode away rapidly.

Tom nodded in the direction The Kid had indicated. "Let's go."

He kept his rifle out, balancing it across the saddle in front of him as they rode.

"My name's Morgan," The Kid offered.

"Tom Lame Deer. I'm the foreman on the Arrowhead 7. My father owns the spread. In case you're wondering about a bunch of redskins dressing like white men and running a ranch, we're Cherokee. Pa came over here from East Texas about twenty years ago."

"I wasn't wondering." The Kid had run into some renegade Apaches in the recent past, but he'd never had any dealings with the Cherokee. He recalled hearing that the tribe was peaceful and had a large reservation up in what was now called Oklahoma.

"My people have always been farmers and ranchers," Tom went on. "That is, the ones who

247

weren't doctors and lawyers and businessmen and teachers."

"Your father wouldn't happen to be a doctor as well as a rancher, would he?"

"No, but if you're telling the truth we can take your Ranger friend to Bandera. There are several good doctors there."

"That's good to hear," The Kid said.

"What happened to your friend, anyway?"

The Kid told the truth. "He was shot in the leg. We were with a posse chasing a gang of outlaws that destroyed a town a good ways west of here. A place called Fire Hill."

Tom Lame Deer shook his head. "Never heard of it. But that doesn't mean anything, I reckon. I never got out that way much."

"The outlaws ambushed us," The Kid went on. "Several men were killed and some others wounded, but Culhane was too bad off to travel. I decided to get some help for him."

"What about the rest of the posse?"

"They went on after Latch."

Tom shot a glance over at him. "Warren Latch?"

"That's right," The Kid said. "You've heard of him?"

"I reckon everybody in this part of Texas has heard of him. If you've got an unruly kid who won't settle down at night, you tell him that if he doesn't go to sleep, Warren Latch will come and get him. Either that or the Devil, and I think more folks are scared of Latch."

"Maybe with good reason," The Kid muttered.

"So this posse chased him all the way from out in West Texas and is still on his trail?"

"That's right."

Tom shook his head. "They must be mighty determined to catch him."

"He destroyed their town and killed a lot of their loved ones, They're not going to turn back. They're not even going to slow down."

That was what worried him more than anything else. With Vint Reilly in command, backed up by Abel Gustaffson and Ed Marchman, the posse might charge foolishly into another trap.

Lace might try to talk some sense into them, but those three would never listen to a woman, even one like Lace. The Kid was convinced of that.

When they reached what The Kid had thought was a creek but was really the Medina River, it didn't take them long to find the spot where he had left Culhane.

The Ranger, who was propped up against a tree as he had requested, with blankets behind his back to cushion him, lifted a hand in greeting as the two riders approached. "That didn't take you long, Kid. Who's that with you?"

"His name's Tom Lame Deer," The Kid explained as he swung down from his saddle.

"His father owns a ranch a few miles from here."

"Lame Deer, eh?" Culhane repeated. "Cherokee?"

Tom nodded. "That's right, sir. Are you really a Texas Ranger?"

"You bet I am. Morgan there showed you my badge, didn't he?"

"Yeah, he did." Tom had dismounted, too. He knelt next to Culhane. "You're shot through the leg?"

"Yeah. Reckon it wouldn't have been too bad if it hadn't nicked somethin' that made me bleed like a stuck hog. This young fella and his lady-friend saved my life."

The Kid started to say something about Lace not being his ladyfriend, but he stopped. He supposed most people would consider that to be the relationship between them. They wouldn't see that what was really going on was much more complicated.

So complicated, in fact, The Kid didn't know what to call it . . . or think about it.

Tom looked up at The Kid. "It looks like you were telling me the truth. I'm glad I sent Chuck back for the wagon."

"Who's Chuck?" Culhane asked.

"My little brother. Also works on the ranch. We all do. There are seven of us in the family. That's why my father called it the Arrowhead 7." Tom gestured at the bandage wrapped around the

Ranger's leg. "You want me to take a look at that?"

"Miss McCall changed the dressin' on it just before she left with the posse, so I reckon it'll be all right for a while longer."

Tom nodded. "We'll have you to the doctor in Bandera in a couple hours." He frowned. "Wait a minute. You said this woman went with the posse?"

"She's a bounty hunter," The Kid said. "She's after Warren Latch."

"And you just let her go? You're supposed to care about her, and you let her go after a man like Latch?"

Anger welled up inside The Kid. "Lace makes her own decisions. Nothing I could have told her would have changed her mind, and if I'd tried to forbid her from going or anything like that, it would have just made her more determined than ever."

"Maybe so, but . . . why didn't you tell her you love her and *ask* her not to risk her life like that?"

The simple question hit The Kid like a punch in the gut. Why hadn't he told Lace that he loved her?

For one thing, he wasn't sure he did. He cared about her, certainly. Cared deeply. But love? He had loved his wife. He didn't know if what he felt for Lace McCall was the same thing.

But he didn't know that it wasn't, either.

251

He ignored Tom's question and changed the subject. "You'll stay here until your brother gets back with the wagon?"

"Sure," Tom Lame Deer replied with a nod. "You're going after the posse?"

Culhane said, "Durned right he is. And he ain't gonna waste any time about it, either. Are you, Kid?"

"No," The Kid said. "If you'll take care of my pack horse, too, I'll come back to your ranch and get it later. If I don't come back, he's yours." He dug around in the pack and came out with extra ammo, then reached for the buckskin's reins. "The trail led southeast?"

"Yeah, toward San Antonio, just like it has for the past few days," Culhane said. "I heard Reilly and them others talkin' about it." The Ranger shook his head. "Never thought I'd see Reilly takin' over like that. I wasn't even sure he'd live this long."

"If he runs into Latch, he may not live much longer." The Kid put his foot in the stirrup and stepped up into the saddle. "So long, Ranger. Tom, I'm much obliged for your help."

"Wait a minute," Tom said. "This gang of outlaws, they're headed for San Antonio?"

"That's what we think."

"I can cut some time and distance off your trail, if you'll trust me."

"You haven't given me any reason not to so far. Which way should I go?"

"Cross the river and follow it for a couple miles. You'll see what looks like a blind canyon. Follow it and you'll find that it's really not. There's a trail at the far end that leads over a ridge. It's pretty rough, but a man on horseback can make it. On the other side of the ridge, turn east again on the trail you'll find there. That'll save you a good five miles of twists and turns that'll slow down a big group. You might even get ahead of Latch's bunch, although I can't promise that."

That sounded like a good plan. The Kid nodded. "I'm obliged to you again, Tom."

As The Kid turned the buckskin, Culhane called, "Good luck, Morgan!"

The Kid lifted a hand in farewell. He was going to need that luck.

A worrisome premonition had started to stir ever since Tom Lame Deer had asked that question about Lace. Even with luck and a shortcut, he wasn't sure he was going to make it in time.

CHAPTER 28

Tom Lame Deer's directions turned out to be good ones. The Kid found the blind canyon without any trouble, and at the far end of it, just as Tom had told him, was a narrow trail that led up a steep, rocky bluff.

The sure-footed buckskin climbed the trail

without The Kid having to dismount. They descended the ridge on the other side and came to the well-defined trail Tom had mentioned. It ran almost due east and west. The Kid turned east.

He hadn't ridden along it very far when he heard gunfire in the distance. The Kid stiffened in the saddle, his heart pounding hard in his chest.

A lot of possible explanations for somebody shooting flashed through his mind, but his gut told him none of them applied except one. The members of the posse were battling for their lives against Warren Latch's gang of ruthless killers.

Already moving at a pretty good pace, The Kid heeled the buckskin into a run and leaned forward in the saddle to urge more speed out of the horse.

The buckskin responded with its usual gallantry, stretching its legs and eating up the ground. Even over the drumming hoofbeats, The Kid heard the gunfire getting louder. Riding around some rocks, he saw that the trail merged with a smaller trail from the northwest. That was the route the others had been following, he realized.

Tom Lame Deer had been wrong about getting ahead of Latch's gang or the posse. Obviously, they were still ahead of The Kid.

Not for long, though. He followed the trail through a couple more bends and spotted puffs of powdersmoke coming from behind small boulders and brush along the base of a bluff to his right.

He reined in for a quick assessment of the layout.

To the left was a much thicker stand of trees, and shots were coming from that direction, too. The sight of several men and horses lying motionless on the ground told The Kid what had happened.

Latch's men had hidden in the trees, and the posse had ridden right in front of them like targets in a shooting gallery. Those who were still alive were pinned down in sparse cover against the bluff, and it was only a matter of time until the outlaws picked them all off.

The Kid pulled back behind some rocks, hoping none of Latch's men had spotted him. He might be able to work around behind them and catch them in a crossfire. Another possibility was circling to the top of the bluff. It would give him the high ground and a better angle for firing at the men hidden in the trees.

Either way, the odds were against him and the posse. As many as half a dozen men had been cut down in the ambush.

Lace hadn't been among the victims. He would have spotted her red hair if she had been hit. Hoping she was still all right, he figured it was just a question of keeping her that way.

Trying to reach a quick decision on his best course of action, time unexpectedly ran out on him. With a burst of fresh shooting, men on horseback suddenly emerged from the rocks and charged straight toward the trees where the outlaws were hidden.

The unmistakable figure of the heavily bandaged Vint Reilly was in the lead.

The Kid bit back a groan of dismay. The posse men never had a chance. Guns roared and cracked, and a wave of lead scythed through the suicidal charge. Men and horses fell, spouting blood from their wounds. It wasn't a fight anymore.

It was murder.

And exactly the sort of foolhardy, revenge-driven stunt The Kid had expected Reilly to pull. The man was too crazed by his need for vengeance to think straight. He was willing to charge right into the guns of Latch's men for a chance to kill some of them, and somehow he had convinced the other men in the posse to go along with him.

Or some of them, anyway. The Kid didn't think all the men had followed Reilly. He still hadn't seen Lace or Nick Burton. Maybe they were taking cover in the rocks and brush along the base of the bluff.

If that was true, they were in a bad spot. The outlaws would probably try to wipe them out.

All the men who had charged the gang were down. A few were only wounded and tried to scramble back to cover, but their bodies jerked grotesquely as more slugs thudded into them. They slumped back to the ground, either dead or dying. A few futile shots came from the members of the posse who hadn't joined the charge, but they weren't enough to provide any cover for their wounded companions.

No bullets had come The Kid's way, so he thought there was a good chance he hadn't been spotted. He wheeled the buckskin and raced back the way he had come, searching for a way to get to the top of the bluff.

He found a path a moment later and sent the buckskin plunging up it. Quickly, the slope became too steep for the horse. The Kid leaped out of the saddle, dragging the Winchester with him, and started up the rest of the way on foot.

Reaching the top of the bluff, he hurried along it, staying low so he wouldn't be skylighted. He stopped at a spot above where the remaining members of the posse were huddled behind the skimpy cover. The Kid went to his belly and thrust the rifle over the edge of the bluff.

He couldn't see the outlaws in the trees, but an occasional glimpse of movement was enough to give him their general locations. Sighting on one, he pumped three rounds from the Winchester, working the rifle's lever with eye-blurring speed between shots.

Without waiting to see the results of his burst, he shifted his sights and fired three times at another spot where something moved. He did that twice more, leaving him with three rounds in the

Winchester. He had fired twelve shots in about as many seconds.

Heavy return fire angled up at the top of the bluff. The Kid pulled in the rifle and scooted back a couple feet. Rocks, dirt, and dust flew in the air where bullets chewed up the rim. Latch's men could shoot like that all day without touching him.

While waiting for the outlaws to get tired of wasting ammunition, The Kid took fresh cartridges from his pocket and thumbed them through the Winchester's loading gate. When the Winchester was fully loaded again, he slid forward, came up on a knee, and swung the rifle from left to right, spraying eight rounds into the trees before he threw himself back out of the line of fire again.

That was enough for the outlaws. A few moments later, The Kid heard a swift rataplan of many hoofbeats across the way. He risked a look and saw dust boiling up on the far side of the trees as the gang fled.

He wondered for a second if it might be a trick, then decided it wasn't. There were too many horses for that. Latch had hit the posse with all the men he had left, and they were all lighting a shuck out of there.

Sliding and bounding, The Kid hurried back down the path to the spot where he had left the buckskin. He swung up into the saddle and headed for the trail that led in front of the bluff. The Winchester was out and ready to fire if he needed it.

As he trotted the buckskin toward the rocks at the base of the bluff, two men ran out from behind them. The Kid swung the rifle toward them for a second before he recognized them as Thad and Bill Gustaffson.

"Mr. Morgan!" Thad exclaimed as The Kid reined in. "Are you the one who ran those varmints off?"

"You know it had to be him, Thad," Bill said. "Who else could it have been?"

The Kid dismounted and let the buckskin's reins dangle. "We'd better check these men. Some of them might still be alive." He started toward the members of the posse who had fallen during the ill-fated charge.

That wasn't the case with the first half dozen he came to. When The Kid rolled Abel Gustaffson onto his back, both of the man's sons groaned at the sight of their father's blood-soaked shirt and sightless eyes. He had been shot at least three times in the chest.

"We told him not to . . . not to go out there," Thad said in a choked voice. "But Reilly said it was the only way, the last chance to settle the score for everything we'd all lost."

"Pa said he didn't care anymore," Bill added. "He just wanted to kill some outlaws. Now he . . . he's . . ."

The Kid left them to their grief and moved on

to some of the other men. They were dead, too, some of them from Fire Hill, others cowpunchers from the M-B Connected.

But he still didn't see Lace or Nick.

He swung around and sharply asked the Gustaffson brothers, "Where's Nick and Miss McCall?"

Bill dragged the back of his hand across his eyes to wipe away some of the tears he couldn't hold back. "Latch has got 'em, I reckon."

The Kid drew in a shocked breath. "Latch?"

Thad nodded. "The posse got scattered when the shooting started. I saw Nick's horse go down, and so did Miss McCall's. I don't think they were hit, though, just thrown clear. Some of Latch's men came out of the trees and got them while the rest of the bunch laid down covering fire. They dragged them back into the trees."

The Kid didn't need any more explanation than that. Latch had seen the opportunity to grab a couple hostages and had seized it. He might not have even realized at the time that Lace was a woman, and he certainly hadn't been aware that Nick was the grandson of a wealthy rancher.

All the luck seemed to have swung back around to Latch's side.

"How many men do we have left?" The Kid asked grimly.

Thad turned and waved toward the rocks. "Come on out, fellas!"

Three men emerged from cover. Two of them were M-B Connected hands. The third man was Ed Marchman, which came as a surprise to The Kid. He'd expected to find Marchman among the dead men. He had already seen Clyde Fenner and Jack Hogan, both of them shot to ribbons.

The Kid started to say something, then decided to let it go. Marchman might not be much good, but at least he was a warm body and another gun.

"Let's round up some of the horses that weren't hurt in the shooting," The Kid ordered. "We don't want Latch to get too far ahead of us."

"My God!" Marchman exclaimed. "You're still going after him? There are only six of us! He probably has three times that many men!"

"I don't care," The Kid said in a hard, flat voice. "He's got Lace and Nick, and I'm not going to let anything happen to them if I can stop it."

"You're crazy," Marchman insisted. "Let's just go to San Antonio and tell the law there what's happened. Let them handle it. That's their job." The storekeeper looked gaunt and haggard. "We've ridden more than a hundred miles, and what's it gotten us? Just a bunch of dead men!"

"It was your decision to come along," The Kid snapped, "just like it was your decision to throw in with Reilly after Culhane was wounded."

"Well, what was I supposed to do?" Marchman blustered. "What would you have done differently?"

"I wouldn't have paraded right in front of Latch's

261

guns without doing some scouting first, for one thing." Disgust welled up inside The Kid as he shook his head and turned away. "Forget it. It's too late to change anything now. All we can do is go after Latch and try to rescue those prisoners."

"I won't do it, I tell you! I'm going . . . home . . ." Marchman's voice trailed off as he realized he didn't have a home or a business to go back to. Warren Latch had seen to that.

The Kid wasn't going to waste time arguing with Marchman. "Do whatever you damn well please. I'm going after those outlaws, and any of you who want to can come with me."

"We're with you, Mr. Morgan," Thad said.

"Damned right," Bill added.

"So are we, Morgan," one of the cowboys said. "The old man would have our hides if we didn't bring Nick back to him safe and sound."

The Kid didn't make any promises.

Bill Gustaffson went on. "Do you reckon we can . . . bury our pa first?"

The Kid shook his head. "Sorry, but there's no time. Not if you're riding with—"

He stopped as a groan came from somewhere among the bodies littering the trail. Swinging around swiftly, he looked for the man who was somehow still alive among the welter of death.

He was shocked to see Vint Reilly pushing himself up on an elbow. Reilly shook his head as if trying to clear it.

Without knowing how he got there, The Kid found himself standing over Reilly, booted feet widespread, the Winchester in his hand pointing down at the bandaged man. Blood seeped from the bullet graze underneath the torn bandage on his head. Reilly had been wounded in the charge and fell unconscious. The outlaws hadn't shot him again because they thought he was dead. The Kid could see all that plain as day.

Reilly looked up and saw the intention in The Kid's eyes. Giving a hollow laugh, he rasped, "Go ahead, Morgan. You think I . . . give a damn anymore?"

CHAPTER 29

"Don't do it, Morgan," Ed Marchman said. "It'd be murder!"

"Murder?" The Kid repeated. "After the way he led all these good men to their deaths? Sounds more like justice to me!"

Thad said, "It might not be murder, but I bet you'd regret it, Mr. Morgan."

"This ain't the kind of thing you do," Bill added.

For a long moment, The Kid stared down at the defiant Reilly. Then he sighed, muttered a curse under his breath, and turned away. As much as he wanted to blow a hole in the loco son of a bitch, the others were right. If he did, he'd regret it later.

Without turning back around he jerked his head toward Reilly. "Somebody help him up."

Marchman hurried to Reilly. "Let me give you a hand, Vint."

Reilly stubbornly ignored him. In obvious pain, he hauled himself to his feet, felt around inside his pockets and produced the little brown bottle of painkiller. "Ahh."

Reilly must have brought several bottles with him, The Kid thought. He couldn't have been nipping at the same one during the entire pursuit.

Taking hold of the buckskin's reins, The Kid mounted up. "I'll catch some of those horses that scattered during the ambush. Get as much ammunition as you can carry and maybe some extra guns."

"Scavenge from the dead, you mean?" Marchman demanded in an outraged tone.

"I can't think of anything better to do with their bullets than using them on the men who killed them," The Kid said.

"Morgan's got a point there," one of the cowboys said. "Come on."

It didn't take long for The Kid to catch six horses and bring them back to the survivors of the ambush. Seven men now, including him, against nearly three times that many.

Oh, well, he mused, the odds had never been good in this pursuit.

"They're less than an hour ahead of us, but

they'll be moving fast," The Kid told the men as they rode out. "We'll have to move faster."

They picked up the trail on the other side of the trees where the outlaws had hidden. After a half mile or so, the tracks curved back to the main trail, which soon ran into an actual road.

"I think this is the road between Bandera and San Antone," Thad said. "I remember coming this way once, a few years ago."

"I think you're right," Bill agreed.

"They'll make better time now." The Kid's hopes of catching up to the outlaws before they reached San Antonio were sinking. The posse could push the horses only so hard without riding the animals into the ground, which would allow Latch and his men to get away for sure.

And he couldn't stop thinking about what Tom Lame Deer had said earlier . . . about what he should have said to Lace before they parted.

The Kid hadn't been a praying man for a long time, but at that moment he was praying that Lace was still all right.

"Squirm a little more, why don't you, darlin'?" Slim Duval told the redhead who was riding double with him. "I don't mind at all."

His arm was wrapped around her waist as she perched on the horse's back in front of the saddle. From time to time his arm slid up far enough to feel the warm pressure of her breasts.

She cursed him with the intensity and creativity of a bullwhacker and added, "Sooner or later I'll kill you, mister. Count on it."

Duval laughed. "I won't hold my breath waiting, if you don't mind."

Latch had already told him he could keep the redhead once they reached San Antonio. The youngster was a different story. Foolishly, he had let slip that he was the grandson of the rancher whose money the gang had stolen out of the stage station safe at Fire Hill.

They had already taken a considerable amount of old Marcus Burton's money. There was no reason they shouldn't have more of it, in the form of ransom for the boy, Latch decided.

Of course, even if the old man paid the ransom, the boy was doomed, Duval knew. Latch would take particular pleasure in blowing the whelp's brains out, probably with one of those fancy foreign guns of his.

The boy was riding in front of one of the other men, looking stunned. As well he should, Duval thought. He was in deep trouble, whether he knew it yet or not.

Duval hadn't been sure about the idea of setting up another ambush for the posse after the previous attempts to wipe them out had failed. But Latch had been insistent, and of course there was no use arguing with him.

And it had worked. A few of those stubborn

bastards might still be alive, but not enough to come after Latch and his men. Whoever was left of the posse could limp back to the ruins of their homes and try to pick up the shattered pieces of their lives.

Duval would have liked one more shot at the man on top of that bluff who had forced them to light out before the massacre was complete, but he supposed that in the long run, it didn't really matter. By the end of the day, whoever was left of the gang would be in San Antonio, and the chase would be over.

And he would have the redhead to amuse himself with for a while, until he grew tired of her and sold her to the madam at one of the houses along the river.

Alongside Duval, Latch startled him a little by saying, "You see, Slim, it's just a matter of proper planning. That's what it takes for a successful operation."

Duval felt a surge of anger. He knew Latch blamed him for the previous failures, but the boss didn't have to rub his nose in it. But all he said was, "You're right, Warren. That ambush you set up went off slick as it could be." He couldn't resist adding, "Too bad we didn't manage to kill all of them."

Latch waved a hand as he rode. "It doesn't matter. There can't be more than two or three of them left alive. They're no threat to us."

Duval felt a little shudder go through the woman he held so tightly. Maybe her lover had been among the men who'd been killed back there. He hoped so. He didn't mind a little spirit in a woman, but if she knew nobody was going to come after her, she would be easier to handle.

Making good time, the gang moved at an easy lope over the road. As they came around a bend, however, Latch abruptly raised a hand to signal a stop. Several hundred yards ahead of them, moving slowly along the road, were a dozen freight wagons.

"Well, well," Latch said as a smile curved his thin lips. "What's this?"

"Nothing we need to bother with, Warren," Duval said. "We can leave the road and get around them. They'll never even see us."

Ignoring his second-in-command's suggestion, Latch took a pair of field glasses from his saddle-bags and lifted them to his eyes. "Those wagons are empty," he reported a moment later. "Just as I expected since they're on their way to San Antonio. The drivers have already made their deliveries . . . and collected the money that was due for the goods they carried."

"Which can't amount to much, compared to the loot we've already got," Duval pointed out. "Holding them up would be a waste of time, Warren, not to mention running a risk that we don't need."

Latch's head snapped around toward him. "You think I'm afraid of a bunch of teamsters?" His voice dripped scorn. "I was *born* to lead men into battle."

"That's exactly what I mean," Duval argued. "Hitting those wagons would be a waste of your time and talents. It's beneath you, Warren."

Latch turned in his saddle to look back along the line of men, less than half as many as had started out a couple of weeks earlier. Their faces were impassive, and none of them said anything. They all knew Latch was half loco. They would do whatever he told them to do.

"Fortune has begun smiling on us again," Latch said. "It wouldn't be wise to turn our backs on fortune's smile."

Crazy as an outhouse rat, Duval thought. Latch was probably hearing voices in his head again.

But he was the boss, no doubt about that.

"You want to hit those wagons, we'll hit 'em," Duval said.

Latch smiled as he stowed away the field glasses and drew his left-hand Mauser. "We'll take our time until we get closer."

"Then we'll hit them, and hit them hard."

"You're gonna die," the redhead said under her breath to Duval.

His arm tightened around her. "Maybe, but you're going to be right in front of me, honey child."

•••

The Kid let the men stop and rest their horses for a few minutes every now and then, but for the most part he kept them moving as fast as he dared.

His eyes constantly scanned the wooded, hilly terrain around and in front of them. He didn't think Latch would attempt another ambush so close to the gang's goal, but if this remnant of the posse rode into a trap, that would be the end of them, no doubt about it.

Their only chance was to take Latch and his men by surprise and kill enough of the outlaws in the first strike to make the odds closer to even.

So when The Kid heard gunfire up ahead, it surprised him. He had figured Latch's bunch wouldn't slow down until they reached San Antonio. But every instinct in his body told him they were responsible for those shots.

The Kid reined in and paused long enough to pull his Winchester from its saddle sheath. He motioned for the other men to do likewise.

"That's got to be Latch. Maybe the gang ran into some trouble. If they did, it's a break for us. We'll see if we can't turn the tide against them. But be careful . . . They've still got Nick and Miss McCall with them."

Unless Latch had decided to kill the two prisoners and dump them somewhere along the way, The Kid thought bleakly. With a man as crazy as the outlaw leader seemed to be, anything was possible.

Reilly said, "Don't worry about . . . those prisoners. Just kill . . . as many outlaws as you see."

"Mister"—Thad turned in his saddle toward Reilly—"why don't you just shut the hell up!" The young man exploded. "You think you're the only one who suffered? The only one who lost somebody? My brother and me lost both our folks and our sisters! And *you're* the one who got my pa killed! You and your beatin' the drums for revenge all the time!"

"Take it easy, Thad," Bill said.

"Easy? Easy! Reilly's as loco as Warren Latch is! We shouldn't have even brought him with us. He'll find a way to get us all killed!"

"No, he won't," The Kid said. "If he tries, I'll shoot him myself. You hear that, Reilly?"

"I . . . hear you. And you don't . . . scare me, Morgan. You can't . . . hurt me."

"We might just see about that," The Kid snapped. He pulled the buckskin around impatiently. "Come on. We're wasting time."

All seven of the men pounded down the road toward the sound of the gunshots.

Several minutes later, they came in sight of a line of freight wagons stopped along the road. Gunsmoke spurted from the backs of the wagons where the teamsters had taken cover behind the thick sideboards. They were firing at men on horseback who raced back and forth, blazing away at the wagons like Indians attacking a train of immigrants.

"That's . . . them," Reilly grated. Digging his heels into his horse's flanks, he sent the animal lunging forward.

"Mr. Morgan!" Thad yelped.

The Kid lifted his Winchester. "For once Reilly's done the right thing. Let's get 'em!"

He urged the buckskin into a pounding run behind Reilly. The other men strung out behind him. The outlaws had their attention focused on the wagons and didn't see the new threat approaching rapidly from behind them.

They had Latch's men in a trap.

The Kid's eyes searched for a flash of red hair, but didn't find it. He didn't see Nick Burton, either. The two of them had to be there somewhere, he told himself. The alternative was unthinkable.

Until he could find them, The Kid could gun down those outlaws without having to worry about hitting the prisoners.

Ahead of him, Reilly opened fire with his pistol before he was in good range, his desire for revenge getting the better of him again. The Kid brought his rifle to his shoulder and sprayed three shots into the gang of outlaws. Even though firing from the back of a running horse played hell with a man's accuracy, he still brought down one of them.

Finally realizing the trouble they were in, some of the outlaws whirled and fired at the charging riders. The Kid snapped two more shots and saw another man throw up his hands and pitch from the saddle. Close enough for handgun work, he jammed the Winchester back in the saddle boot and palmed out his Colt.

The teamsters had put up a lot stouter defense than Latch had expected. They had downed some of the outlaws already, and as dust roiled and shots roared, The Kid and his companions brought down more. The fighting was fierce, but not without paying a price. The Kid saw Vint Reilly jerk in the saddle as a bullet punched through his burned body. He stayed on his horse and charged straight toward two outlaws, still firing as he thundered toward them. He was hit again and then again, but he kept going. The outlaws finally broke in fear of the bandaged apparition coming toward them with a roaring gun in his hand.

It was too late. Reilly blasted them off their horses before he tumbled off his own mount and rolled over and over on the ground.

The Kid whirled the buckskin and triggered another shot that tore into the throat of an outlaw. Blood flooded over the front of the man's shirt as he clutched futilely at the wound before losing his balance and falling from his horse.

Turning the buckskin again, The Kid saw that Ed Marchman was down . . . but not dead. He pushed himself up and fired his pistol at the remaining outlaws. Marchman might be a jack-ass, but at that moment, he didn't lack for courage.

Thad and Bill Gustaffson were right in the middle of the fight, too, their rifles cracking as they fired shot after shot. They fought with a fierce intensity. Not loco, like Reilly, but clearly determined to avenge the deaths of their loved ones.

Then, suddenly, it was over. The shooting stopped. All the outlaws were down. The rugged-looking teamsters emerged from their wagons, carrying their rifles. "Are you men Rangers?" one of them called to The Kid.

"No, but we're what's left of a posse that's been on the trail of these outlaws," The Kid explained. "This was Warren Latch's bunch."

"Latch!" the man exclaimed. Like seemingly everyone else in that part of the country, he had heard of the outlaw leader. "You mean we actually beat Warren Latch's gang?"

"That's right." The Kid nodded. He looked over the dead outlaws. "But I don't see Latch himself among them. He must have lit out when the attack didn't go like he expected it to."

Not all the outlaws were dead, The Kid realized as one of the bloody figures on the ground suddenly coughed and rolled onto his side.

Instantly, half a dozen rifles covered the man.

The Kid quickly dismounted and motioned for the men to give him room. With his Colt still in his hand, he knelt next to the wounded outlaw. "Who are you, mister?"

"S-Slim Duval," the man gasped out. He looked like he'd been shot at least twice in the belly. He didn't have much time left.

So this was Slim, The Kid thought, the one who had led that scouting party they'd run into a few nights earlier.

"Where's Latch, Duval?"

"I . . . I don't know. He . . . ran out on us. We never . . . turned on him . . . no matter how loco he got . . . and then he double-crossed us!"

"Then you won't mind telling me where to find him," The Kid said. "You had a couple of prisoners, a woman and a young man—"

"Latch took them . . . with him . . . along with . . . all the loot. I never . . . never thought he'd do something . . . like that."

The Kid grunted. "No honor among thieves, eh? Tell me where to find him. Where does he go in San Antonio?"

Duval's voice rose into a despairing wail as he replied, "I don't know!"

"Well, you'd better think hard." The Kid put the revolver's barrel under Duval's chin and pressed it into his throat as blood leaked from a corner of the outlaw's mouth. "Because if you can't help me find Latch and those prisoners, I don't have any reason not to kill you right now."

CHAPTER 30

San Antonio was beautiful at night. The lights of the sprawling city stretched for a long way.

Downtown, along the river, and near the ruins of the old mission called the Alamo, music and laughter drifted through the open doorways of the numerous saloons. The warm night air was filled with the scent of flowers, although the stink of decay from the river lay underneath the more pleasant smells.

The house was built in the Spanish style, with a red tile roof and an adobe wall around it. A black wrought-iron gate opened into a garden.

The Kid didn't try to open the gate. He went over the wall, dropping lightly into a shrub-bordered flower bed on the other side.

His black trousers, shirt, and hat helped him blend into the darkness. The Colt's handle with its ivory grips was the only bit of light about him, and he had his hand wrapped around it. Somewhere not far away, a guitar played a mournful tune.

A balcony with iron railings overlooked the

garden. As The Kid approached stealthily, he heard a door open. Pausing in the shadow of a thick shrub, he knelt and looked up.

A man stepped out onto the balcony and walked to the railing. He rested one hand on the rail, and the other lifted a cigar to his mouth. As he took a deep drag on the cigar, the coal at its end glowed brightly, casting a faint light over his face.

From the darkness below, The Kid saw the lean features, the jutting beard, the deep-set eyes. He knew without being told that he was looking at Warren Latch.

The outlaw leader wore a pair of military-style holsters. The odd-shaped butts of the guns were visible in the light spilling through the open door behind him.

The pistols were some sort of foreign make, The Kid guessed, since he had never seen anything quite like them before. It didn't matter. Latch could have a damned Gatling gun and it wouldn't matter.

One shot would have ended it simply. From where The Kid crouched, he could have put a bullet through Latch's head and the man would never know what ended his life.

But The Kid didn't know where Lace and Nick were. If he killed Latch and then searched the house, only to find that the prisoners weren't there, he would be at a dead end.

No, Latch got to live a little while longer . . .

until he told The Kid what he wanted to know.

Latch stood there smoking his cigar for several minutes, then dropped the butt, ground it out under a booted toe, and kicked it off the balcony into the garden. He turned and went back into the house, closing the door behind him.

The Kid stole forward swiftly and silently.

The pillars supporting the balcony had enough scrollwork to provide a few handholds and footholds. His privileged childhood in Boston hadn't afforded him opportunities to climb trees that most boys got, but he was able to manage. He struggled up one of the pillars until he could reach over his head and grasp the iron railing.

From there it was easy to pull himself onto the balcony.

A couple large windows glowed a warm yellow with lamplight from the room where Latch had gone. The Kid crouched and tried to peer through a corner of one. A gauzy curtain covered the window.

He was able to see a little through the loosely woven curtain, and could tell Latch was standing in front of someone sitting in an armchair. That close to the window, he realized it was raised a few inches to let in the night breezes.

The first thing he heard sent a thrill shooting through him. It was Lace McCall's voice. "—get away with this, you son of a bitch."

"That's where you're wrong, my dear," Latch

replied. "No one knows where I am or the name I use while I'm here in San Antonio. This house belongs to Stephen Dandridge, the somewhat decadent but law-abiding son of a wealthy businessman from Louisiana. I've put quite a bit of time and effort into cultivating that identity."

"And nobody ever notices that you look like Warren Latch?"

"A lot of men are tall and slender and have beards. Besides, people see what they expect to see."

"Well, what are you going to do now?"

"If you're worried that I'm going to molest you, you needn't be. My interests along those lines are few and rather . . . specialized. But I know several men who will be quite taken with you. I thought I would invite them over and have them, ah, place bids on the pleasure of your company."

"You're going to auction me off like a horse?" Lace sounded like she couldn't believe it.

"Between what I make from you and the ransom I expect to get for the young man locked up downstairs, I should clear a nice bit of money. Since I no longer have to share the other loot I brought back with me, I'll have a small fortune to sustain my lifestyle for an extended period of time."

"Which you got by double-crossing your men," Lace said scornfully.

"I think my friend Slim was getting a bit tired of riding with me, and to tell you the truth, I had grown tired of him. As for the others . . . well, they were just common outlaws. I can round up a hundred more like them if I ever decide to form another gang. After all . . . I'm Warren Latch. Everyone wants to work with me because I'm always successful. And everyone is afraid of me because I'm insane, you know."

The laugh that came from Latch made a chill go through The Kid, as he suddenly realized it was all an act. Latch didn't sound the least bit crazy. It was fake, just like the identity of Stephen Dandridge that he had established. Warren Latch, the mad dog . . . Don't cross Warren Latch, he's loco . . . He'll kill you as quick as look at you.

All a lie to cover up pure evil.

The Kid had heard enough. Gun in hand, he stepped to the door and kicked it open.

Latch whirled, hands going to the butts of his guns, but he stopped short as he found himself staring down the barrel of The Kid's Colt.

"Kid!" Lace cried. "He told me you were dead, but I didn't believe him! I never did." Her hands were tied tightly in front of her. Another rope around her waist bound her to the chair. An ugly bruise stood out on her jaw.

At that moment, The Kid came very close to pulling the trigger and killing Latch.

But he held off. If Lace was the one who turned

Latch over to the law, she would get the reward for him. That's what she had set out to achieve, and The Kid was going to make that possible if he could.

"You're from that posse!" Latch gasped in astonishment.

"That's right," The Kid said. "You didn't wipe us all out. Half a dozen more are on their way in, but I raced ahead to settle things with you."

Latch's surprise seemed to be wearing off. He actually smiled as he asked, "How the devil did you find me?"

"Slim Duval wasn't quite dead when we caught up to him."

Latch shook his head. "Slim didn't know where I live or the name I use here."

"No, but he knew how to get a message to you. He knew about the girl who works at Flores' Cantina, who knew about the liveryman, who knew about the priest, who told me about the man named Dandridge who always makes generous contributions to the mission. It wasn't that hard to find you, once Duval started me on the right trail."

Latch's face hardened with anger. "He's dead, you say?"

"That's right."

"Good." Latch practically spat. "He used to be a good man, but he'd gotten sloppy, lazy. He had it coming."

The Kid ignored that and asked, "Lace, are you all right?"

"Yeah. I've been knocked around a little, but I'm fine."

"How about Nick?"

"Tied and gagged in the pantry off the kitchen downstairs. He's all right, too, as far as I know. That arm wound may need some attention."

"It'll get plenty of attention soon. Can you get loose?"

"I don't think so. I've been trying to loosen these ropes, but the knots are too tight."

"When I've finished with Latch, I'll cut you loose."

A smile curved Latch's thin lips. "You're finished now, my friend."

"I don't know how you figure that," The Kid said.

"A wise man knows how to spend his money. I've spent some of mine on men whose job it is to keep an eye on that girl at the cantina. If anyone comes around asking her the wrong sort of questions, they follow and find out who it is." Latch nodded toward the door. "They're standing behind you now."

The Kid shook his head. "You don't really expect me to—"

"Kid, look out!" Lace screamed.

Instinct sent him twisting down and to the side. Guns roared behind him, and he felt a bullet tug at his shirt sleeve. From the corner of his eye he saw two men on the balcony, one white, one Mexican. Flame spurted from the barrels of their guns.

A slug tore into the expensive rug only inches from The Kid's hand as he braced himself and fired. One of the men doubled over as the bullet punched into his belly.

The other man weaved to the side as The Kid triggered again. The shot missed.

Another weapon roared, the reports coming so fast and so close together they blended into a roll of gun thunder. Bullets chewed up the rug as The Kid rolled desperately away from them. Latch had yanked out one of his funny-looking pistols. Flame licked from its muzzle as he fired again and again.

Even on the move, The Kid got off a shot that smashed into the chest of the man on the balcony and drove him halfway around before he collapsed. That took care of two of the three threats, but Latch was the most dangerous of all.

The boss's gun ran dry, but he already had the second pistol in his other hand. Before he could bring it to bear, Lace drew up her legs and kicked him in the back of the knees. Latch cried out in surprise as his legs folded up beneath him and he fell. The pistols slipped out of his hands and fell, clattering to the floor.

Lace couldn't get out of the chair, but she threw

herself forward with such desperation it toppled with her. She fell onto her side and reached for one of the guns Latch had dropped, snatching it off the rug just as he grabbed the other gun and rolled back to his feet.

Did he have the empty one, or did she?

The clicking of the gun as he frantically jerked the trigger answered that. In the next instant, the pistol Lace held in both hands roared. One after another, the bullets thudded into Latch's chest, their impact driving him backward in a grotesque dance. She kept shooting as he stumbled onto the balcony, crashed into the railing, and toppled over it, falling out of sight into the garden.

Up and on his feet, The Kid started toward Lace, but she cried, "I'm fine! Make sure he's dead!"

That seemed like a foregone conclusion to him, as many times as Lace had shot the man, but she was right. The smart thing was to be certain.

Gun ready in his hand, The Kid went onto the balcony and checked first on the two men he had shot. They were dead, sure enough. And when he looked over the balcony railing, he saw Warren Latch lying on his back on the flagstones of a patio below. A dark pool of blood spread around him.

"Is he dead?" Lace called from inside the room.

The Kid lined his sights and fired a shot that blew the top of Latch's head off.

"No doubt about it."

• • •

The Menger Hotel, one of the finest hostelries in San Antonio, was practically next door to the Alamo. The Kid and Lace were sitting in its lobby a week later when Asa Culhane came through the front doors and thumped toward them using a cane. Nick Burton was with the Ranger.

The Kid got to his feet to shake hands with Culhane. "You look like you're getting around pretty well. Better than I expected, as bad a shape as you were in."

"Yeah, well, I'm a tough old bird. I heal fast." Culhane inclined his head toward Nick. "Like this youngster here."

Nick's wounded arm was in a sling, but his color was good, and he seemed to be feeling fine. He was dressed in a town suit. "Ranger Culhane called me and told me he was coming over here to see you, Mr. Morgan. I thought I'd come along so I could say good-bye to you and Miss McCall."

Nick and Culhane sat down in a pair of comfortable armchairs facing the sofa where The Kid and Lace sat.

"You're headed back to your grandfather's ranch?" The Kid asked.

"That's right," Nick replied with a nod. "Thad and Bill are going with me. They decided they didn't want to try to make a go of their family's ranch after everything that happened there, so they're going to let that neighbor of theirs pay them off for it." The youngster grinned. "I told them there were jobs waiting for them on the M-B Connected, if they wanted them."

"Won't that be up to your grandfather?" Lace asked.

"No, ma'am . . . I mean, Miss McCall."

"Lace," she reminded him.

"Yes'm . . . I mean . . . well, you know what I mean. But as for what you asked me, no, I reckon if my grandpa plans on me taking over the ranch, it's high time he starts giving me some responsibility. And me hiring Thad and Bill is a good place to start. If he doesn't like it . . ." Nick shrugged.

"I've got a hunch he'll like it just fine," The Kid said with a smile.

"I hope so, Mr. Morgan."

"I think after all we've been through, you can call me Kid."

"I don't know . . . After reading those dime novels about you, it seems sort of . . . disrespectful."

The Kid laughed. "Don't worry about that."

Culhane asked, "Did you get that reward money all right, ma'am?"

"I did," Lace told him. "I've already sent most of it back to my mother."

"You plan to keep on bounty huntin'?"

"It's the only thing I know," she replied in all seriousness.

The Kid and Lace had spent most of the past week in the Menger's finest suite, paid for by Conrad Browning's money, resting and recovering and getting to know each other better. On more than one occasion during that time, The Kid had brought up the subject of Lace giving up bounty hunting, but she had always dodged the question.

He knew she didn't want to give up the life she had made for herself, despite its dangers, and in truth, he couldn't blame her for feeling that way.

He had done the same thing in his own life.

"Then I reckon there's a chance our trails will cross again sometime," Culhane said. "I'm goin' back to active duty with the Rangers as soon as this leg o' mine heals up. In fact, it's really Ranger business that brought me here today."

"Chasing another fugitive?" The Kid asked.

"You could say that," Culhane replied. "There's an hombre I'm after."

He reached inside his coat for something, and when he brought out his hand and extended it, a silver star on a silver circle lay on his palm. It was a Ranger badge, but it wasn't the one belonging to Culhane. That badge was pinned to his shirt.

"I talked to my cap'n, and he agrees with me," Culhane went on. "This is yours if you want it, Kid. What do you say?"

Center Point Large Print
600 Brooks Road / PO Box 1
Thorndike, ME 04986-0001 USA

(207) 568-3717

US & Canada:
1 800 929-9108
www.centerpointlargeprint.com